INISH

Inish
Bernard Share

Dalkey Archive Press
Champaign and London

Library of Congress Cataloging-in-Publication Data

Share, Bernard.
Inish / Bernard Share. -- 1st Dalkey ed.
p. cm.
ISBN 978-1-56478-541-1 (pbk. : acid-free paper)
I. Title.
PR6069.H335I55 2009
823'.914--dc22
                        2008050070

Partially funded by a grant from the Illinois Arts Council, a state agency,
and by the University of Illinois at Urbana-Champaign

www.dalkeyarchive.com

Cover: design by Danielle Dutton, illustration by Nicholas Motte
Printed on permanent/durable acid-free paper and bound in the
United States of America

INISH

1.

I TRIED to hand it to him as casually as possible. It's a thing you don't study in school, handing things casually when they are never handed any other way but casually, and you couldn't offhand or casually think of the way to hand them uncasually. The dialogue presented a problem but I managed to balance it muzzily on a kind of souvenir-fulcrum, you won't see one of these again for a long time and so on, although if I had wanted to stretch it I had brought along an extending-ladder of allusion which would take me up to 'in case they run out of toilet paper', as if in a ship this size that could ever be a funny or even a sensible remark.

He took it well, with a grin and an underhand motion which whisked it neatly under his right arm, paper reaching armpit as cigarette returned to mouth, another of those unplanned movements which some furry ancestor must have practised for days with a bone and plantain leaf. All around little onanist rituals were taking place, some squashing sorrow, some summoning sorrow, some saying love to the kids and eyeing five inches of nylon that someone else was exposing on a bar stool. The native women were packing up their trinkets, the scarves and squares and dress-lengths, and preparing to disembark. My timing, for a lousy timer, hadn't been all that bad, but I had to get away now before there was any risk of that paper boomeranging, before there was a chance of his laying it down, negligently, and forcing me into some impossible position such as don't forget to read the racing results or there's a picture of Hackett on page five, as if he cared a damn about Hackett or what had won tomorrow's big race. The page I now wanted to forget, page eleven, would perhaps come burbling out of me instead: Don't miss the . . . on page eleven, I would cry foolishly, and for that he would certainly think me more than mad and leave it on the table for the steward who would glance at it, see that it was unamerican and shovel it into one of those cardboard boxes of old turnips that seem to go over the side with stupid regularity when you're two or three days out.

It was time, at last time to be going, and I wound myself up for the last of the farewell speeches we'd been making to one another for the last twenty-nine days. Nothing grand of course, no gestures—between men you have to put it all into a handshake and a kind of sideways look which shuffles big emotions in square brackets from eye to eye. He was draining his gin now, and I suddenly noticed the deepening lines on his cheek and the black-pepper pattern of stubble, things you're always supposed to be noticing if you're observant or a woman but that I never register in the ordinary way of things. Well, it's been good, Allen, he led off, or it was some simple banality like that. I quickly gave it him back: have a good trip, you old bludger, write, love to (mentioning the four or five names it was still possible that we had in common), and my love to ——, conjuring up for his benefit my fading images of the hotels we had once drunk in, the old unfamiliar places. There's no way out of this sort of thing, but only the natives of this island seem to be any good at it without embarrassment and with unabashed verve. There were two of them at it over there in the corner, a father and daughter perhaps (the artificial atmosphere of the ship makes such judgments difficult) but they were literally on one another's necks, shedding real first-water tears, and she was grinding the toes of her shoes together as if honing them to lacerating points. The loudspeaker started saying All persons not travelling please board the tender through the entrance on B deck, and though it would probably say it again I used this statement as my springboard, muttered a last well-that's-it, at this point it might just as well have been Búsquelas en nuestras tiendas, and dived down the crowded stairs (three cases Cabin Class Big Letter H—Hood, Horne, Hughes?— blocking everyone's way) before he had time to make a reluctant offer to see me off, as if walking the last few hundred yards of corridor (is that the right word for a ship's passageway?) would have any effect except spoiling the flavour of his glass of arrack and the remnants of my composure.

The gangway was midships (that's right), and the canvas sides to it were flapping horribly, the officers mounting guard holding their hats on in the wind funnelling up as if frozen into an obsequious forelock-touching posture. I had forgotten how unpleasant the weather had been when I came on board three hours ago, and I had forgotten until now how much arrack we had drunk out of the bottle in his cabin. Now the mixture of hot-air-conditioning and cold sea wind hit me in the stomach like a blow from the handle of a push-pull suburban lawnmower when it jams on one of the dog's bones and a square of bare planking loomed up at me as I doubled forward, cleared and ready to receive my offering. I fought back, won by a hairsbreadth—the prickly bile taste had washed my back teeth—and began lurching down the striated ladder in the hopes that the movement would keep the alcohol moving centrifugally rather than operating like a lift-pump. When I came out of the covered gangway onto the deck of the tender it was cold, raining and nearly dark. He's well away I thought as a last tribute to the man in the bar, and putting my hand into the pocket of my raincoat, touched the reassuring bulk of tomorrow's paper.

•————————————————————————

"I'll teach the cat to spell and then there'll be no such thing as a mouse any more", the small, sou'westered child in the lee of the deckhouse was solemnly telling his sister, or it might have been his aunt—the artificial atmosphere of the ship makes such judgments difficult or perhaps there had been one of those confusing overlaps of generations that you sometimes get on this island. The tender was slurping up and down the ship's side with a most evil sound. The deckhands were still netting and swinging up the last of the cargo, the mailbags now, their slow talk bouncing off the job at a tangent, turning to verbal confetti on the wind. The sour smell of the engines began to mix unpleasantly with the gin and arrack and what was left of the hot-air-conditioning. I found myself a wet, slithery patch of slatted bench on the windward side—there is a certain fascination in nautical vocabulary—though the big ship was sending the draughts in all directions, and, closing my eyes, tried for an easy takeoff into suspended animation, hands on pullover inside raincoat through double pockets, one containing the reassuring bulk of tomorrow's paper, ankles crossed as if chained, neck sunk into collar like a broken lead soldier mended with a matchstick. My last glimpse of that world was the grey, distant coast of the island, just like any other in the rain. I missed the five inches of nylon, which, coming down the gangplank in the wind, became seven and a half inches and

2.

ALL this will happen tomorrow, when the boat sails. The paper will be there because the paper is here, in front of me; the man will be there because he is called Allen because it begins with an A; the seven and a half inches will be there because they are always there, you can look straight through a skirt at them, and anybody's children, even Allen's, can talk about cats if they use the appropriate Inish phonemes. The difficult piece is where I hand him the paper. How am I really going to do it? Am I going to be careful enough to carry tomorrow's paper from here to there, to hand it to him as casually as possible, it's a thing you don't study in school, handing things casually when they are never handed any other way but casually and you couldn't offhand or uncasually think of a way to hand them uncasually. The dialogue will present a problem but I will manage to balance

it muzzily on some kind of souvenir-fulcrum, you won't
see one of these again for a long time and so on, you won't

This is an import-export business. I have been in this
island, in the import-export business, for four years next
March 29th, next March being a leap year. I like that, it
has pared down the anniversaries to a needle-sharp four-
faceted point (you couldn't call it an anniversary), something almost druidical in its precision. All over my desk,
all over tomorrow's paper, is all the stuff that I've just
peeled off the Mexican consignment. All the creations of
MAYA DE MEXICO bear great originality of design or of
the materials employed, whether they be cotton textiles
or fabric, whether they be cotton textiles or cam-
baya. Look for them at our chain of shops. Todas las creaciones de MAYA DE MEXICO tienen la gran originalidad del
diseño o de los materiales que se usan son bloody crook
as usual but I bring them in for the gimmick value not the
quality. Búsquelas en nuestras tiendas in every city and
town in all the variegated provinces of this island, worn
by the native aristocracy and distinguished

I bring a lot in for the gimmick value. Witness the variegated wrappers on my desk on tomorrow's paper: Jamsan
jokilaakson elimenellisena yhddistajna. Entirely new floor
show CHEQUERS 183-195 Pitt Street Sydney BL 4586, liquor
must be ordered before 9.30 p.m. Published weekly at
Keflavik airport, Iceland. Deadline for copy: 9 a.m. Monday. Telephone number 4156. Pierre Bernard, ancien rédacteur en chef (1936-1946). And there underneath them,
when I have peeled off the wrappings and thrown the
goods away, is tomorrow's *Times*, they call all these local
rags the *Times*, and I had scarcely read the first word (be-

ginning with an A for a prominent position) when Allen interrupted.

• ────────────────────────────────────

This is an import-export business. I try to handle this paper-work as casually as possible. It's a thing you don't study in school, handling things casually that are never handled any other way but casually and you couldn't off-hand or casually think of the way to handle them uncasually, but I have to try when I peel the wrappings off the latest batch of MAYA DE MEXICO bear greatest originality of design o de los materiales que se usan and throw the goods away and get down to the paper-work. Off they go, to nuestras tiendas in every city and town in all the variegated provinces of this island and I sit back in Keflavik airport, Iceland (Pierre Bernard, ancien rédacteur before 9.30 a.m. Monday; liquor must be ordered at Jamsan jokilaakson, Pitt Street), and try to teach the cat to spell in unimpeachable Inish phonemes so that there'll be no such thing as a mouse any more. I wait until five inches of nylon, coming down the gangplank into the wind, becomes seven and a half inches and (hands inside raincoat through double pockets, ankles crossed as if chained) and thus keep the paper-work at bay, saying this is now my island, this is still my island until next March 29th, next March being a leap year, something almost druidical in its precision. There's paper-work and paper-work of course (this dialogue presents a problem but I manage to balance it on some kind of muzzy souvenir-fulcrum). There's on the one hand Keflavik airport, Jamsan, Pierre Pitt (must be ordered before 9.30 a.m.) and on the other tomorrow's *Times*, they call all these local rags the *Times* . . . but this is an import-export business.

This is a funny little island. Their government pays me money to come and set up in business and watch their antics. They talk about the judicial murder of George Plant in the language of their oppressors and die for the right to import other people's customs and other people like me, an import-export agent with the machinery of government in the first-floor workroom to qualify for the foreign manufacturers' grant. There's paper-work of course—Pierre Keflavik at BL 4568 gives me a hand with that—but otherwise I just bring in a lot for the gimmick value and sell it en nuestras tiendas in every city and town. The first time I showed the departmental official my residence permit he took it well, with a grin and an under-hand motion which whisked it neatly under his right arm, paper reaching armpit as cigarette returned to mouth, another of those unplanned movements which some furry ancestor must have practised for days with a bone and a plantain leaf. So I became without much difficulty and in the course of time an import-export agent, learning in the newest version of my newest language the lore of un-sheathed auger flighting. That was after one year and so I was not quite correct in saying that I have been in this island, in the import-export business, for four years next March 29th, next March being a leap year. I like that, it has pared down the anniversaries to a needle-sharp four-faceted point, and I was putting it like that to myself when I was interrupted by Allen before I had scarcely read the first word in tomorrow's *Times*, they call all these local rags

I was reading in tomorrow's paper, here in my import-export business, the advertisement I am putting in when Allen interrupted and demanded that I begin at the be-

ginning. I have been in this island for four years. I have
been in the import-export business for three years next
March, so Allen belongs at the beginning, ancien rédacteur en chef. I tried to hand him the paper as casually as
possible. It's a thing you don't study in school, handling
things casually when they are never handed any other
way but casually and you couldn't offhand or casually
think of a way to handle them uncasually. Have a good
trip, you old bludger, I said, conjuring up for my benefit
his fading images of the hotels we had once drunk in, the
old unfamiliar places. But he looked at me strangely before draining his gin—nothing grand, of course, no gestures—and I remembered the farewell speeches we'd been
making to one another for the past four years, next March
being a leap year. He wanted to be put in first because
he wanted to be gone, he wanted to leave it on the table
for the steward who would glance at it, see that it was
unamerican and shovel it into one of those cardboard
boxes of old turnips that seem to go over the side with
such stupid regularity when you're twenty-nine days out.

●————————————————————

8.06 / 8.36 / 9.06 / 9.41 / 10.06 / 11.36 / 12EO6 / 1.06 /
1S36—so they used to stop on their way out to the sea.
And over there on the up side: 7.10 / 7.45 / 8.13 / 8.37 /
9.12 / 9.39—they must have been for the businessmen, the
old businessmen who grew decrepit with their trains until
at last both died together. It was natural that when I first
saw the rusting black nameboard recapitulated below in
picturesque Inish characters I should misread it as ARRACK
MINE (the rust was essaying a pincer movement) but
Hackett quickly put me right. Mr. J. Hackett had a knack
of handing around small bits of local knowledge as inof-

●

fensively as cigarettes, and advised me on what to say to tomorrow's *Times*, they call all these local rags the *Times*:

STATION SOLD BY PRIVATE TREATY

Mr. Ecks, a successful Amnesian businessman, is reported to have bought the old Arrack Mines station, which was closed to all traffic x years ago next March 29th, next March being a leap year. It is understood that he intends to convert the premises for use as a plant to manufacture Amnesian Arrack for export, and is negotiating with Bord an tAma for a grant under the Underdeveloped Stations (Miscellaneous Decisions) Act, 1936-1946. When asked about the potentialities of the export market Mr. Ecks declined to comment, pending the complication of certain informalities.

Mr. Ecks looked out from the old stationmaster's old office, thumbing the tattered timetables he had found in forgotten corners and sentimentally souvenired. The abandoned platforms, through which no trains came regularly at 8.06 / 8.36 / 9.06 / (down) and 7.10 / 7.45 / 8.13 / 8.37 / (up) were already sown with smugwort, swineherd's fennel, hickory and lesser anodyne. The sweat that told of the effort to convert the premises for use as a plant to manufacture Amnesian Arrack for export still beaded his swarthy Amnesian brow. He was perhaps forty, perhaps not, a fine, tall, stocky figure of a man, slightly bald and greying a little over his aristocratically pallid temples, his thick shock of strong chestnut hair combed in a jaunty quiff over his thick, strong, jaunty right eyebrow.

"Yes", he said in his attractive Amnesian accent to the cub reporter who was growling at the litter on the floor, "Yes", he said, handing him a cigarette as inoffensively as a small bit of local knowledge, "you may say that I am very happy to have come to your so beautiful country with its charming natives so ready for soaking, its beautiful and virtuous maidens so ready for jeopardizing, its blue mountains and its purling latreens running pure gold". He paused to adjust his tie, which was hanging on a defunct gas-pipe by his imposing roll-top desk. "I have no intention, of course, of imposing my roll-top desk upon your so beautiful country with its charming, its beautiful, its purling without giving something in return. I shall offer employment, deployment, decoyment and dénouement to your charming natives ready for soaking, beautiful and virtuous maidens ready for . . .".

Here another of the reporters present (not from this newspaper) went off with a loud bang. Mr. Ecks again turned and looked out of his darkening stationmaster's window. The 5.45 p.m. train from the city had not just stopped and disgorged its usual complement of old businessmen who had grown decrepit with their trains. His particular friend, a Mr. H. Jacet, whose gravestone he had come across when poking around in the local churchyard, greeted him with a nod of his umbrella and a wave of his head.

"Grand evening!", he mouthed through the dusky stationmaster's window.

"Grand Duchess!", Ecks mouthed back in deference to Mr. H. Jacet's well-known predilection for nicer people. He turned to check the train on his salvaged timetable. As usual it had not departed at 6.06—exactly on time.

Dismissing the tale-chasing cub reporters from his old stationmaster's old dusky office, he looked around him at the evidence of his honest enterprise. "This is an import-export business. I have been in this island, in the import-export business, for four years next March 29th", he ruminated loudly to himself, "next March being a leap year. I like that", he said more loudly through the stationary window to Mr. H. Jacet, by whose efforts the purling latreen on the platform was now running pure gold, "it has pared down the anniversaries to a needle-sharp, four-faceted point, something (he paused to light his gas-pipe on which his tie was still hanging) almost druidical in its precision".

"Grand piano!", Mr. H. Jacet, buttoning his fly, mouthed through the dusky stationmaster's window.

"Grand Canyon", he mouthed back, watching Mr. H. Jacet going off bang, as he didn't do every evening, to one of the nicer houses, with a nicer wife, nicer children and nicer au pair girl (a man after her own heart) in one of the nicer roads in Arracker Mines.

Relaxing at his imposing roll-top desk Mr. Ecks averted his gaze from the dusky stationmaster's window and tried to hand himself the paper as casually as possible. He had just read the piece in tomorrow's *Times* headed STATION SOLD BY PRIVATE TREATY and was now trying not to read, further down the same page, Allen's last message that he had dictated before catching the boat tomorrow. The text, from the preface to Sir John Daniel's *The Philosophy of Ancient Britain*, read as follows:

MEN BECOME INSANE
—College Lecturer

A college lecturer once declared from a public platform that he had known men become insane through the study of Druidism, and that the system was a heathen and impossible one. By those who share his opinion my temerity in investigating such a dangerous and intolerable subject

15

may be regarded in a very uncomplimentary light; but this does not deter me from attempting to lift the veil that has covered Druidism for centuries, for I am persuaded that, like the opening of Egyptian tombs, something may be disclosed worthy of our admiration. What I may advance may be "to the Jews a stumbling block, and unto the Greeks foolishness", but to others it may bring to light long buried treasures of wisdom.

He was draining his arrack now, and I suddenly noticed the deepening lines on his cheeks and the black-pepper pattern of stubble, things that you're always supposed to be noticing but that I never register in the ordinary way of things. He had tried to hand me the paper as casually as possible, and in a few minutes he would mutter some excuse in a cadence that was still too careful for a native Inish speaker and disappear down towards the entrance on B Deck. All persons not travelling please board the tender. Had I, I wondered as I drained my own gin into the deepening stubble of black pepper, had I forestalled him? Or was Sir John Daniel perhaps a little premature? My mind wandered back four years, or four years it would be next March 29th, next March being, of course, a leap year, to the first day I showed him Arrack Mines, as he quickly called it, and hinted at its suitability as a station which used to boast of a regular and reliable service, with the occasional non-stop boat train to provide the necessary and compensatory grandeur. It was, in fact, a grand evening when we inspected the premises. "But this is an import-export business", he joked, fingering the tattered timetables he had unearthed in the old stationmaster's old office, rubbing a pudgy hand over the dusky window overlooking the up or down line. I ex-

plained to him Sale by Private Treaty, translating carefully into rather old-fashioned Amnesian.

"Todas las creaciones de MAYA DE MEXICO tienen
la gran originalidad!", he agreed—enthusiastically, I
thought at the time—and we spoke of other things. Now I
am seeing the last of him; having dealt him my Daniel-
blow and he, in his turn, handing me the paper as casually
as possible, tomorrow's *Times,* they call all these local
rags the *Times.* When we are three days or so out I will
open it and read—an appeal that I may or may not heed
depending whether the five inches of nylon have by that
time become seven and a half or seven and a half plus
suspenders, thigh, more nylon, kisscurls and the rubber
silence of ships' corridors in the straining night. I will recall, perhaps between parted lips, how four, no three,
years ago next March 29th Arrack Mines station became
through the courtesy of Bord an tAma an import-export
business managed by Pierre Bernard, ancien rédacteur
en chef, and that all liquor was ordered before 8.06 / 8.36 /
9.06 /9.41 /10.06 / 11.36 / 12EO6 / 1.06 / 1S36. I know I
am the first on the list, the first to be given the paper as casually as possible, because in a way I am the last, the last
stop before the station; and to save time and trouble, and
to get back as quickly as possible to the seven and a half
inches suspenders, thigh, kisscurl, rubber silence, parted
lips I had better, perhaps before leaving it on the table
for the steward who will glance at it, see that it is unamerican and shovel it into one of those cardboard boxes
of old turnips, make my deposition. For though I took it
well, with a grin and an underhand motion which whisked
it under my right arm, I was conscious of the unplanned
movements of furry ancestors, of something almost dru-

idical in its precision, and the thought occurred to me, between the five and seven and a half inches and in the straining silence, that since I had been more than partly responsible for the Sale by Private Treaty I could not honourably turn my back on the 7.10 / 7.45 / 8.13 / 8.37 / 9.12 / 9.39 . . . and that perhaps I shouldn't have got in first with Sir John Daniel.

You will have gathered, my broads, babies (o those phonemes!) and pencilmen, that in the person of Mr. Allen I am a sensualist and an escaper. In the person of Mr. Ecks, an Amnesian businessman of uncertain provenance and doubtful authenticity, I set myself up in the deserted station of Arrack Mines, ostensibly to become an import-export agent dealing in unsheathed auger flighting and other objects of art and virtue originating in Keflavik airport, MAYA DE MEXICO, Pitt Street, Sydney, and Jamsan jokilaakson elimenellisena yhddistajna. This is all, of course, a big cover up, as my friend Mr. H. Jacet, when he has finished buttoning his fly, will be happy to tell you. My real purpose in buying Arrack Mines station was to continue in the comfort and homeliness of my own convenience my studies, begun in farthest Amnesia so many years ago now, into the long-buried treasures of wisdom, though I was fully aware that investigating such a dangerous and intolerable subject might be regarded in a very uncomplimentary light. The mission, I regret to say, failed, a college lecturer having declared from my public platforms that he had known men become insane through the study of druidism, and that the system was a heathen and impossible one. Thus, after having been in this island, in the import-export business, for four years next March 29th, I shall be obliged to take ship tomorrow for further foreign parts, handing myself the paper as casually as possible and refusing to answer any questions until I am safely ensconced between seven and a half inches of nylon. Only then, the ship being three days out and having prevented the steward from shovelling it into one of those cardboard boxes of old turnips that seem to go over the side with stupid regularity, will I be able to take the paper neatly from under my right arm, turn to page . . . and read (beginning with an A for a prominent position) the first word of the advertisement.

•————————————————————

This is all, of course, a big cover-up, as my friend Mr. H. Jacet, when he has finished buttoning his flies one by one to the ceiling of this duskily-shaded room, will be happy to tell you. No, Allen the Amnesian businessman has not yet left and I have not yet tried to hand him the paper as casually as possible (it's a thing you don't study in school) because the paper, tomorrow's *Times*, they call all these local rags the *Times*, is on this rumpled bed in front of me, and I am trying now to turn to page . . . and read (beginning with A for a prominent position and for Allen because it begins with an A) the first word of the advertisement.

Let me tell you about this myself, before Mr. Ecks or Mr. H. Jacet with a nicer wife, nicer children and nicer au pair girl come back one by one on to the ceiling of this duskily-shaded room. Let me tell you how Mr. Ecks came to leave me tomorrow with a copy of the paper (I took it well, with a grin and an underhand motion which whisked it neatly under my right arm); let me tell you why the nicer Mr. H. Jacet says "Grand Duchess" whilst buttoning his fly; and let me tell you why I am lying on this bed looking up at the ceiling of this duskily-shaded room, the telephone beside me not ringing its not-number BL 4586, whilst outside in Pitt Street the sinuous green trams grind past on their way over the Harbour Bridge to Clontarf—or do you go via the North Strand? And why I have beside me a copy of a noble work of English literature which shall be nameless but which is most certainly not the preface to Sir John Daniel's *The Philosophy of Ancient Britain* (COLLEGE MEN BECOME INSANE—Lecturer) and a pile of novels of inferior quality in point of literary merit from which I have selected a number of passages now marked by strips torn from the pages of tomorrow's *Times*.

It is because (with the trams of Pitt Street outside and the not-telephone BL 4586 beside me) that I do not understand English very well that I have the pile of novels of inferior quality beside me from which I have selected a number of passages instead of only the noble work of literature that shall be nameless. One of the first things that I learnt when I began working for Mr. H. Jacet was that unusual fluency was essential to the composition of pornography, for which he pays me well in Amnesian pounds, redeemable on the sinuous green trams that grind over the Harbour Bridge to Clontarf. I speaka da language, you see, read it more than well enough to read the advertisement in tomorrow's old Arrack Mines Timestable, but to write it! Ah! (gives New Australian shrug of shoulders, mutters in outlandish Old Amnesian dialect. Why don't you New Aussies bloody well speak English, says man in Pitt Street tram. No-hopers! Dills! Drongos!). But as I was saying, before Mr. Ecks, with another of those

●

unplanned movements which the man in the Pitt Street tram must have practised for days with a bone and a plantain leaf, so abruptly interrupted me: the dialogue, as I was saying, presented a problem, but for a time I managed to balance on some kind of muzzy souvenir-fulcrum. Thus I equipped myself, closing my eyes, trying for an easy take-off into suspended animation, with remembered fragments from my old Amnesian days, such as: s'envoyer en l'air avec une femme, se faire secouer le panier à crottes, mettre la tête à l'étau, souffler dans le poireau, téléphoner dans le ventre, tailler une plume, se faire dauffer. I tried to handle it as casually as possible, but it's a thing you don't study in school, the pornographic transliteration when you no speaka da English verra well et il est interdit by all dinkum Aussies de parler Amnésien.

So though I tried to hand it to Mr. H. Jacet, buttoning his fly, as casually as possible he understood that the dialogue presented a problem, even though I had tried to balance it on some kind of souvenir-fulcrum, and he suggested what about a pile of novels of inferior quality, sport, to help you with that noble work of English literature which shall be nameless but which is most certainly not, mate, the preface to Sir John Daniel's *The Philosophy of Ancient Britain* (MEN BECOME INSANE COLLEGE LECTURERS) because the bludgers wouldn't buy it anyway, the no-hopers, the dills, the drongos!

Now it is all really very simple, since Mr. H. Jacet, buttoning his fly, handed it to me as casually as possible. What we end up with is something which looks like a noble work of English literature which shall be nameless but thanks to she was so slim that it was almost as easy to take her from behind as face to face while she kicked up

INISH

one foot in its blunt-toed black shoe as a gesture of play-
ful resistance or simply wanton freedom et elle semble
heureuse de se déshabiller devant un homme et une
femme sa combinaison tombe à côté de sa robe et elle
enleva son slip et speeka da English, mate, and her lips
opened once more beneath mine, my hand began its slow,
greedy descent, taking in, conquering (the dialogue presents a problem) the smooth miracle of her flesh, then my
fingers encountered that first capricious little curl and I
tried to handle it as casually as possible but sometime it
would recall to me, on the ceiling of the duskily-shaded
room, the five inches of nylon which, coming down the
gangplank in the wind, became seven and a half inches
and

That was the system, as outlined to me, mouthing
through the dusky Pitt Street stationmaster's window, by
Mr. H. Jacet. Into that noble work of English literature
which shall be nameless but which is certainly not the
preface to "Insane College Men Become Lecturers", by
Pierre Bernard, ancien rédacteur en chef, I was to insert
from my pile of novels of inferior quality in point of literary merit the passages marked by strips torn from the
pages of tomorrow's *Times*. For example: she didn't answer, she merely stooped, unbuttoned her shirt (skirt? I
no speaka da English verra well) and stepped out of it,
she was wearing brief white panties almost transparent,
his hand trembling he turned off le corps de la fille. Je
lui avais même déboutonné la robe par derrière (no-
hoper! dill! drongo!) et j'avais, à travers le col, atteint
ses seins, quoique this did not deter me from attempting
to lift the veil that has covered Druidism for centuries,
for I am persuaded that, on the opening of the noble work

of English literature that shall be nameless, something is disclosed worthy of our admiration, in other words a newly-minted gem of pornographic literature, masquerading under the guise of a noble work of literature that shall be nameless but will command a ready sale, búsquelas en nuestras tiendas, in every city and town in all the variegated provinces of Australia. This, sport, said Mr. H. Jacet, buttoning his fly and handing me a pile of novels of inferior quality and a copy of tomorrow's *Times,* is an import-export business. I import your talent for pornography even though you no speaka da English verra well, you no-hoper, you dill, you drongo, and export a noble work of English literature which shall be nameless but which now contains brief white panties almost transparent, almost as easy to take face-to-face as from behind her shirt (skirt?). His hand began its slow, greedy descent, taking in, conquering the sinuous green trams, the duskily-shaded room, the telephone beside me not ringing its not-number BL 4586, and, his lips opening once more beneath mine, he began slowly to hand me a copy of tomorrow's *Times* in which he expected me to insert an advertisement beginning . . .

●————————————————————

Now every evening, rain or shine, Mr. H. Jacet, who had not alighted from the 5.45 p.m. from the city which had not stopped punctually at 6.06 p.m. at Arrack Mines, would stroll leisurely along the leafless or leafy avenues of the trim suburb towards one of the nicer houses which contained his nicer wife, nicer children and nicer au pair girl (for Mr. H. Jacet prided himself on his cosmopolitanism) with tomorrow's paper always furled immaculately in his right hand and his umbrella tucked under his arm as casually as possible. This was a matter of breeding, Mr. H. Jacet reflected as he pushed open the gate of his nicer house with its nicer wrought-iron nameplate KEFLAVIK AIRPORT (a sentimental reminder of the delightful honeymoon he and Mrs. H. Jacet and their nicer children and nicer au pair girl had spent in Pitt Street, Sydney, reading to one another from a noble work of English literature which shall be nameless and listening to the sinuous green trams grind past one another on their way over the harbour bridge to Clontarf—or do you go via the North Strand?). He was not now, of course, as young as he was then, and after eating his nicer dinner with his nicer wife he would potter about in his garden among his choice hysterias and glowing hydrants or perhaps take a short walk down the leafless or leafy avenues of Arrack Mines to take a glass or two with his friends Mr. Allen and Mr. Ecks, simple men like himself whom he would entertain from time to time with stories of his vicarious experiences in many parts of Arrack Mines, particularly in the Pitt Street area where, rumour had it, he used to write pornography for his old friend and trusted colleague, Pierre Bernard (1936-1946).

"I don't do much of that sort of thing nowadays, lads", he would admit as Mr. Ecks set them up for the third time, "but since you're both in a manner of speaking interested in the subject you may care to hear a bit of a little story I was putting together for Mrs. H. Jacet and my nicer children and nicer au pair girl. Well yes, just one for the road then, thanks very much".

The three friends always chose a quiet corner of Shenanagan's Lounge Bar where a discussion of a serious nature could generally take place undisturbed. Sometimes their talk would turn to the cultivation of hysterias and hydrants, in which the three friends vied with one another in friendly rivalry, sometimes they would argue about the relative comfort of the 6.15 p.m. from the city, which did not stop at Arrack Mines at 6.05, compared with that of the sinuous green trams of Pitt Street, sometimes the difficulties of the import-export business and particularly the uncertainty of supplies from MAYA DE MEXICO, which, though they bore great originality of design or of the materials, were not really suitable for advertising in tomorrow's paper. This particular evening, however, old Jacet was on his pet hobbyhorse, pornography, and so the three friends settled themselves down comfortably over their glasses (though of course earlier in the evening they had been drinking pints) while Mr. H. Jacet unfolded his manuscript.

"I don't go in much for this sort of thing nowadays, lads", he admitted, "but since you're both in a manner of speaking interested . . . well, here goes". And he began to read in his rather attractive Amnesian accent which was so well known and admired in Arrack Mines:

"A college lecturer once declared from a public platform that he had known men became insane through the study of Druidism, and that the system was a heathen and impossible one . . ."

"And he never spoke a truer word", put in Allen.

"She was wearing brief white panties almost transparent", Mr. H. Jacet continued, lowering his voice, "but this did not deter me from attempting to lift the veil which has covered Druidism for centuries. Her lips opened once more beneath mine, my hand began its slow, greedy descent, taking in, conquering the smooth miracle of her flesh, then my fingers encountered that first capricious little curl".

"Good on yer!", Mr. Ecks chimed in, a little unnecessarily. Mr. H. Jacet looked at him a little reprovingly over the edge of his glasses, which were not yet empty.

"What I advance may be to the Jews a stumbling block", he continued, "but elle semble heureuse de se déshabiller devant un homme et une femme. Sa combinaison tomba à côté de sa robe et elle enleva son shirt. My temerity in investigating such a dangerous and intolerable subject may be regarded in a very uncomplimentary light, mais j'avançais lentement sur le corps de la fille. Je lui avais même déboutonné la skirt par derrière et j'avais, à travers le col. . . .

"Yes?", his two companions chorused together, stiff with excitement.

Mr. H. Jacet coughed.

"Well the next bit is a little rough, lads . . . as a matter of fact it's an advertisement".

Allen pushed away his glass. "Ah now, enough is enough", he said. "I'm as broad-minded as the next man, but that's laying it on a bit thick".

Mr. Ecks pushed away his glass. "Ah now, enough is enough", he said. "I'm as broad-minded as the next man, but that's laying it on a bit thick".

"That's laying it on a bit thick", chorused Allen and Mr. Ecks, pushing away Mr. H. Jacet's glasses, "we're as broad-minded as the next men, decent Inishmen the pair of us, but that's laying it on a bit thick".

Mr. H. Jacet tried to hand it to them as casually as possible. "It's an advertisement", he assured them, "in tomor-

•

row's *Times*. They call all these local rags the *Times*", he offered in explanation.

"Times gentlemen please, it's gone the Times", the voice of Shenanagan broke in: "now gents PLEASE".

His timing for a lousy timer hadn't been all that bad. When he came out of the covered gangway on to the deck of the tender it was cold, raining and nearly dark. They're well away, he thought as a last tribute to the men in the bar, and putting his hand into the pocket of his raincoat, touched the reassuring bulk of the paper.

3.

ANYONE (they always set the first word in capitals) was a good way to begin. There is a chance they might put it in first, though in the Personal Column of course it goes rather by size and importance— a government appointment, or owing to the death of Mr. Ecks, late of Import-Export, Arrack Mines, the offices in Pitt Street will be closed until 2.30 this afternoon. ANYONE POSSESSING INFORMATION . . . it's a good way to begin, even if they only set the first word in capitals, possessing information is something to lure the avaricious, the fact-packed, the word-hoarders, the onanistic correspondents who are always writing to the *Times*. Several times recently I've read letters in the newspapers on the question of modesty in dress, mostly concerned with women's apparel and modern fashions. Many and varied protests are seen from time to time from women (or girls) who maintain there is nothing wrong with the scanty skirts, very short shorts, plunging necklines and other "fashions" being adopted by some—repeat some—of our young women.

Does the climate of this country force young women to don shorts, some of which are so revealing as to be little better than a swimsuit? Hardly. Is a woman any the more charming or graceful for a backless dress, or a daringly low neckline, at a dance or a party? The opposite is often true. So we must look further for a motive and we do not have very far to look. The main motive behind this unnecessary economy of dress material is attraction by sex-appeal and there is far too much emphasis on this method of attracting attention at the present time. Any tendency to immodesty in dress is a step in the wrong direction. Excuses in favour of such fashions can be readily seen for what they are—an attempt by unthinking or notice-seeking women to justify the wearing of objectionable attire.

Next we come to their faces (or luminous dials). What a horrible prospect these so-called charm schools seem to be promoting for girls—each with eyebrows shaved off, and new ones painted on, each with identical mouth shapes, superimposed on their greasy faces. What a grotesque sight they must be each morning. Thank goodness we still can find a few attractive girls in rural country areas who can thoroughly outshine their painted sisters from cities and towns.

That will amuse them on the ship tomorrow, when I have whisked the paper neatly from under my right arm, read the advertisement as casually as possible, ANYONE possessing information, unfortunately not ANYONE POSSESS-

ING INFORMATION, and then turned to see what other souvenirs of the island and its variegated natives can be culled from this copy of tomorrow's *Times,* as they call all these local rags.

Fond memories will, of course, linger freely as I roam the banks' and companies' reports, nary a word of Import-Export and my hardworking but hopeless friend Mr. Ecks, the Amnesian businessman. It was some years since I had seen him—not since that evening in Keflavik airport, all brown panelling and dusty display cases that looked as if they were never opened—when by some strange quirk of fate our planes miscarried simultaneously and we stretched our legs together in the cold, soupy bitterness of the Icelandic autumn afternoon. He wasn't looking well then, I thought. Nor particularly prosperous either. Why else would one go out of one's way to travel via Iceland to America other than to save a few pounds on the fare? He told me about the import-export business he was running in some place called Arracker Mines—you've struck gold? I said by way of a joke but it didn't even get a smile—his English still wasn't so hot and I don't suppose he appreciated the play on words, though I thought it rather witty at the time. He had to go off to Mexico to do a deal over some stuff—cotton textiles or fabric or something—which he said he was bringing in for the gimmick value not the quality.

He seemed very nervous and depressed—perhaps he was worrying about his plane. I thought, well you can't have it both ways, cheap transport and all the latest in aircraft, but no, he said it had been very comfortable until then and he was looking forward to a good sleep. We stood looking out the door of the draughty terminal at

•

the lights of the big army camp winking beyond. There was scarcely a soul about, and this was the deadest international airport I'd ever seen, Mascot included. Then, of course, it struck me. Last time we'd met—in Sydney, Australia, when I was attached for a while to the staff of Professor H. Jacet—he had talked about this book he was writing, and how he was hoping to go to Europe to get ahead with the research. The trouble was, that was about all I could remember about the subject, except that it had perhaps some sort of archaeological or anthropocentric bias. (I recall his quoting Voltaire: Je souhaiterai que vous ressembliez toujours à vous-même). He had a funny title for it, this I remember: MEN BECOME INSANE— sounded more like a cheap thriller than a serious work of scholarship. My own belief was that it was all a cover-up and that he was really tied up in some shady racket or other: he always had a queer, fishy look in his eyes and I was sure at one time the Loftledir ground hostess was going to come over to us and say to him: "Pardon, Monsieur, mais vous me déshabillez des yeux". I left him shortly after that on some pretext (you can't sustain the effervescence of a chance meeting, even up near the Arctic circle) and it was a real surprise to see you, Mr. Ecks, again in this island and do remember me to Mrs. H. Jacet and your nicer au pair girl and be careful going down the gangway in the wind.

That was many years ago (four years next March 29th, next March being a leap year) and now here I am in this bar on this ship, taking the paper from him with another of those unplanned movements which some furry ancestor must have practised for days with a bone and a plantain leaf, and all around me little onanist rituals are taking

31

place, some squashing sorrow, some summoning sorrow, some saying love to the kids and eyeing five inches of nylon that somebody else is inadvertently exposing on a bar stool. It was time, at last time to be going, and he wound himself up for the last of the farewell speeches we'd been making to one another for the last three years.

"Well, it's been good . . .", he led off, and I couldn't help noticing the regret, perhaps the envy in his voice. Here was I, Mr. Ecks, the successful Amnesian businessman, off on another of my transatlantic tours, whilst he, poor old Allen the import-export man, sat at home waiting for the 6.15 from the city not to stop and carefully wrote for himself the advertisement for tomorrow's paper which begins ANYONE possessing information on the . . . and hands it to me as casually as possible, it's a thing they don't teach you in school, having stored up an extending-ladder of allusion which would take him up to in case they run out of toilet paper (that could never be a funny or even a sensible remark) because whatever happens I must begin at the beginning (beginning with an A for a prominent position) and shovel it into one of those cardboard boxes full of old turnips before he has left the ship and the station and Pitt Street and Keflavik airport and the five inches of nylon which, coming down the gangplank in the wind, will almost certainly lift the veil which has covered Druidism for centuries.

•

4.

ATTRACTIVE semi-detached family residence of character on bus route, convenient to shops, schools, churches. Accommodation comprises: Entrance porch and wide hall, large lounge, diningroom, four family bedrooms, bathroom, kitchen and pantry. Outside there is a good greenhouse, fuel store, toilet and garage. The beautifully-kept garden at the rear enjoys quiet seclusion.

This substantially-built house is in good structural order and the rooms are lofty. The auctioneers recommend it as an easily-run, compact family residence. It is held under lease for 150 years from 1929 at the very low ground rent of £5-5-0 per annum. Valuation £32.

•————————————————————

That is not the kind of advertisement I am trying to write, though I can do it quite simply, quite quickly, quite easily by thinking of my nicer wife, nicer children and nicer au pair girl. In the front porch, seven inches (now that I no longer think in metrics) from the edge of the front step there is the front bumper (fender?) of an articulated lorry (truck?) manufactured in moulded polyurethane, coloured red (poly WHAT?), making an angle of thirty-seven degrees, reading from the outside of the step looking inwards, with the line of the tiles. The front door is open, because it is a warm summer evening, though winter in Pitt Street. Three feet inside the front door, in the wide hall, the rear portion of an articulated lorry manufactured in moulded polytruck, coloured variegated blue, lies in the far right-hand corner (looking inwards from the door) of a red and blue hand-knotted woollen rug. In the kitchen and pantry my nicer wife, anticipating my hunger, is preparing the evening meal. In two of the four family bedrooms my two nicer children are asleep. In the third of the four family bedrooms my nicer au pair girl is pretending to write a letter home to Hermosillo but is in fact admiring herself in the full-length mirror. To do this she has taken off most of her clothes and will shortly remove the rest as she is intending to take a bath. I am outside, moving casually between the good greenhouse, fuel store, toilet and garage, and the beautifully-kept garden at the rear which enjoys quiet seclusion, hoping to catch a glimpse of my nicer au pair girl removing the rest of her clothes before taking a bath.

It is a perfect early insular evening. In my garden which enjoys quiet seclusion there is a magnificent display of choice hysterias, glowing hydrants, delicate clitoris. From the kitchen and pantry comes the evocative aroma

•

of curmudgeon cooked in its own juice with a leaf of
spandrel and a pinch of rime. I am at one with this perfect
early-insular evening, I feel attractive, semi-detached,
redolent in the convenience of shops, schools and
churches, prepared to hold my compact family and com-
pacter au pair girl under the lease for 150 years, prepared to see the very low ground rent for the further cultivation of choice hysterias, glowing hydrants, delicate
clitoris. But this is the product of an advertisement I
didn't try to write, an advertisement for an attractive semi-
detached family with an attractive semi-detached au pair
girl whom I could enjoy in the quiet seclusion of the
kitchen and pantry, in the wide, easily-run toilet.

If I had written it then, those four long leap-years ago, I
would have written myself away from Pitt Street, Keflavik
—away from MAYA DE MEXICO búsquelas en nuestras
tiendas. Away from the five inches of nylon become seven
and a half and. I would have taught the cat to sing for the
benefit of my two nicer children (o those phonemes!) who
would have been four and two, or four and three, or two
and one, or one and a comfortable position on top of my
nicer wife smelling comfortably of the evocative aroma of
curmudgeon cooked in its own juice with a leaf of
spandrel and a pinch of rime. I, H. Jacet, would very carefully have avoided having anything further to do with Mr.
Ecks, the successful Amnesian businessman, or with Mr.
Allen, whom I should never have attempted to see off on
the boat tomorrow, nor tried to hand the paper as casually as possible. Alighting regularly from the 5.45 p.m.
train from the city I would have perhaps mouthed "Grand
evening!" through the dusky stationmaster's window, but

no more. And never, of course, would I have become insane through the study of Druidism, nor attempted to lift
the veil that has covered Druidism for centuries, for I am
persuaded that, unlike the opening of the Egyptian tombs,
nothing may be disclosed worthy of our admiration.

That is why, I am now telling myself, as I sit in my nicer
early-insular home with my nicer wife, nicer children, and
bathing au pair girl, that I am trying to write this advertisement as casually as possible, and why, having got as
far as ANYONE POSSESSING INFORMATION ON THE LIFE
(though they only set the first word in capitals) I must
stop again for Mr. H. Jacet.

● ————————————————————

Mr. H. Jacet claimed, in a statement read to the court,
that it was on account of the nicer au pair girl that he was
unable to proceed with his projected study of Druidism,
and in fact that the quiet seclusion of his family residence
was regularly disturbed by her habit of taking off most of
her clothes to admire herself in the full-length mirror and
thereafter removing the rest preparatory to taking a bath.

Mr. Justice Ecks: How much time will be required for
this case, Mr. Allen?

Counsel for the Prosecution: I understand, a Bhrei-
theimh, that Mr. Jacet is conducting his own defence. I
think we might allow a period of four years, counting from
last March 29th.

Mr. Jacet: I object, Your Breitheimh! I intend to call
witnesses from Pitt Street, Sydney, Keflavik airport, and
MAYA DE MEXICO.

Mr. Justice Ecks: These places are not within the juris-
diction of the court and I shall require legal proof of their

existence. Please keep your voice up: the jury must be able to hear every word you say, and I must insist that all persons not travelling tomorrow leave the precincts of the court. Please begin, Mr. Allen.

Counsel for the Prosecution: Miss Nicer O'Pair Girl, please.

Clerk of the Court: Take the Philosophy of Ancient Britain in your right hand. Raise it and repeat after me: "I swear in my nighty, that the evidence I shall give, shall be unto the Greeks foolishness, but to others, it may bring to light long buried treasures of wisdom". What is your name?

Witness: Nicer O'Pair Girl, your Arrackship.

Mr. Justice Ecks: You may stand up, sit down, or lie down as you wish. But please keep your clothes up and undress for the jury.

Counsel for the Prosecution: Miss Girl, you are employed in the attractive semi-detached residence of character belonging to Mr. H. Jacet?

Witness: Yes, your Boatship.

Counsel: And in the course of your duties, you have at times found yourself alone with the defendant in the kitchen and pantry, large lounge, good greenhouse and four family bedrooms?

Defendant: I object, m'lud! Miss Girl cannot have been alone if I was present. And besides, there are the nicer children!

Mr. Justice Ecks: I will allow that objection. Please confine your questions to matters directly concerned with the case, Mr. Allen.

Counsel: I apologise, m'lud. Miss Girl, have you on more than one occasion taken off most of your clothes and

37

removed the rest before taking a bath?

Witness: I have, your Advertisement (sensation in court).

Mr. Justice Ecks: I will not tolerate these interruptions! If they continue I shall clear the court of any stain upon the character of the defendant. Please proceed, Mr. Allen.

Counsel: No further questions, m'lud.

Mr. Justice Ecks: Does the defendant wish to cross-examine?

Mr. Jacet: Yes, Your Breitheimh! Miss Girl, will you please undress as clearly as possible: the jury over there must be able to see everything. Now, where were you on the night of the 29th of March? I must warn you that your particulars may be taken down and used in evidence against you.

Witness: On the night of the 29th of March, Your Dishonour, I was taking off most of my clothes and removing the rest before taking a bath in the attractive semi-detached family residence of character on bus route held under lease for 150 years by Mr. H. Jacet (whom, I might say, I do not see in court).

Mr. Jacet: What occurred, Miss Girl, when you had removed the rest of your clothes before taking a bath?

Witness: I was severely jeopardised by the defendant, your Midship (sensations).

Mr. Justice Ecks: Can you suggest any motive for this alleged attack?

Witness: Sex, your Salaciouship. In all considerations of this problem of pornography we must first get rid of the idea that it is a personal problem only—"the inadequacy", as Trignant Burrow calls it, "of the view which posits a sick individual as over against a well society". Pornography, like delinquency in general, is a social problem and it can only be solved by methods that involve social psychology—group analysis and group therapy. Of this truth psychoanalysts, from Freud to Burrow and Klein, have provided irrefutable evidence. The cure, if there is to be a cure, will involve every normal activity from breast-feeding to the moral and political structure of the state. It means a complete reorientation of the aims and methods of education. Attempts to deal with the problem in any more isolated fashion are either ignorant or hypocritical.

Mr. Justice Ecks: Does the defendant wish to address the court?

Mr. H. Jacet: There is little I wish to say at present, m'lud. Except that anyone possessing information on the life and writings of . . .

Counsel: I object, Your Special Noticeship! Events which have not yet occurred cannot be admitted as evidence in this court. We have already had to listen to a reading of an excerpt from a projected study of Druidism which, I maintain, will never be written, not to mention a section at tedious length from a certain timetable which, I protest, is valid only from 23rd June until 14th September incl., or until further notice. Copies of the Bye-Laws and Regulations will, as your Lordship knows, be found exhibited at the Stations, and, furthermore, a booklet showing the conditions upon which Tickets, including Season Tickets, are issued, and the Regulations and Conditions applicable to passengers' luggage, can be obtained free of charge from the booking office. The defendant, m'lud, is attempting to mislead the court and jury by handling these papers as casually as possible!

Mr. Justice Ecks: Your objection is upheld, Mr. Allen.

In these circumstances I have no alternative but to request you to wind yourself up for the last of the farewell speeches we've been making to one another for the last three years. Nothing grand, of course, no gestures—between men you have to put it all into a handshake and a kind of sideways look which shuffles big emotions in square brackets from eye to eye. I shall give no direction as to costs. Case dismissed.

He has bored me for years, his nicer wife and nicer children, his nicer au pair girl, his attractive, semi-detached, beautifully-kept garden which will grow choice hysterias, glowing hydrants, delicate clitoris but not the kind of advertisement I am trying to write. It's a thing you don't study in school, getting further and further away from something you want to do by careful planning, using dead objects as totems in the hope of transubstantiation, placing your feet carefully up and down curbstones, peering at a glacier of waste ice at the back of the iceworks in the hope that someone will have silvered it and that this time you will see reflected long-buried treasures of wisdom. This time it was the nicer au pair girl. In this island I might have lifted the veil that has covered her for centuries, but once again I read about her in the *Times*, they call all these local rags the *Times*, before I saw her. Further and further I got away from her by careful planning, by watching her as she merely stopped, unbuttoned her skirt and stepped (shirt and stepped?) out of it, she was wearing brief white druids almost transparent et j'avançais lentement sur le corps de la fille. Je lui avais même déboutonné la robe and revealed the inadequacy of the view

which posits a sick individual as over against a well society. The cure will involve every normal social activity
from Freud to Burrow and Klein, but it has once more
eluded Mr. H. Jacet and his nicer au pair girl.

"Is she hot stuff, but?", asked Mr. Allen, bending con-
spiratorially over his glasses. "Them continentals are all
hot stuff".

Mr. H. Jacet tried to hand it to them as casually as possible. "She's an advertisement", he assured them, "in tomorrow's *Times*. They call all these local rags . . . ", he
offered in explanation.

She is there now, the last, O pray the last of her line. If
I turn the page now she will take off her clothes to admire
herself in the full-length mirror and thereafter remove the
rest preparatory to taking a bath. And tomorrow my last
glimpse of the world, of the grey, distant coast of the
island (just like any other in the rain) will be the five
inches of nylon, which, coming down the gangplank in
the wind, will become seven and a half inches and

5.

I f I'm to get this advertisement written and into the *Times,* clear up all this mess, teach the cat to spell and catch the boat tomorrow I'll have to look sharp-ish. Break it down, mate, I said to Jaco (how he hates be-ing called Jaco but then all these New Australians are the same—why can't they speak English like the rest of us), break it down, I can't stand here bloody well talking to you all bloody night. Got a boat to catch. No sheila is go-ing to make me miss that boat. I'm a man of action—Syd-ney today, Keflavik tomorrow, MAYA DE MEXICO the day after—I can't stand here grogging on when there's busi-ness to be done. Now, let's see, how far have we got . . . Christ, you could at least have sharpened the bloody pen-cil, you'd think we were beyond the black stump, and

that's a dinkum Aussie pun for you if ever there was one.
Now, let's give it a go:

ANYONE possessing information on the life and writings
of

Yeah, she'll do. But fair go, mate. Your timing, for a lousy
timer, isn't all that bad, but you just can't leave it at that.
Remember how I stuck by you, mate, when you didn't
know the Hawkesbury from a handsaw. Remember the
cold beers, Tooheys Old, we drank together in those pubs
near Central Railway when I taught you the old Australian proverb: mate equals might and the twin legs of
the broad Australian A straddle king and bastard alike.

Yes, I suppose it was something like that. Australian,
ex-Amnesian Mr. Allen (if I remember him correctly)
was a sport, O every inch a sport; he could drink his
schooners if he had to but preferred middies, liked his
beers long and cold and his sheilas quick and easy.
It might have worked—too right it might. It was growing over him like a comfortable marsupial skin complete
with pricked-up cocky ears, alert for those endless triphthongs sliding away to the invisible horizon: yeeeaaaaaa-
ah—and a pouch in front for every unconsidered trifle.
But it was difficult to find an off-the-peg New Australian
personality that really fitted. The intonation, up at the end
of the phrase, kept taking it back to French as it was pa-
raded by elderly, old-fashioned Amnesians, so that
Monsieur Allain sometimes became a parody of himself,
you have ze cigarette, mite, no? Ooh-ah, oo-la-la. But it
still might have worked, too right it might. He learnt to
watch the sun revolve backwards, to listen to the chatter

in the delicatessen shop as if it were all just bloody foreign, guten morgen, signorina: sbohem. And the children of friends growing up into a new mythology, god save the queens of the drive-in cinema, the flowers that bloom in the spring rolls to take away. Some of them, the friends, may still even answer the advertisement. "You remember Mr. Allen, Anna? Here's something about him in the paper. It says . . .".

What would it say to them about a man whose business they never quite understood? Something in the rag trade, was it? Yes, he was always grogging with—oh, you know, those dills who drive around with the back seats of their Holdens full of girls' dresses. And girls too, of course. Yes, and he had an offsider whom he used to go and see in Pitt Street, seemed to be a real cobber (you will notice how they pepper their talk with the Authentic Antipodean Insular article, to show that they have successfully leapt from the old to the new?) but I was never too sure whether it was the rag trade or some kind of literary work —you know: writing or something. He spoke English well, too. You know, English like they speak it in England— that bloke from the Uni. told me. Yes, you remember Allen —though I just can't seem to remember. . . .

But you must remember in order to answer the advertisement. You must remember every detail, the crack like a broken ray of lightning on the right side of the right shoe of his David Jones slip-ons, where the mould used to grow like fungus when the humidity went up. You must remember the Woodley's Est he used to drink, diluted with lollywater, because the name EST EST EST seemed so perfect a statement about nothing. You must remember the rocks running into the ocean at Dee Why over which he walked one Sunday in his David Jones slip-ons and ruined them with sea water because they (the rocks, of course, not the shoes) reminded him of the road that ran down and away from Keflavik airport, a crater cracked by the cold, and that reminded him of the stone blocks that were coming apart in the Museo in Hermosillo, Mexico (búsquelas en nuestras tiendas) and reminded him of the weeds, the smugwort, swineherd's fennel, hickory and lesser anodyne, that were even now forcing themselves between the granite blocks at the edge of the down platform of Arrack Mines station where the 5.45 p.m. from the city had not just stopped and disgorged its usual complement of the old business.

You must remember all this if you are to compose a proper letter in reply. But facts alone will not satisfy the examiners and opinions must be supported by relevant quotation. You must try to hand it to him as casually as possible, the dialogue will present a problem but if you try to balance it muzzily on some kind of souvenir-fulcrum, you haven't seen one another for a long time and so on, avoid using the extending-ladder of allusion at which point all words are equivalently meaningless anyway. Only in this way, my dear antipodean and mega-insular erstwhile friends, can you be sure that your answers will have any value for him, imprisoned as he is in his attractive, semi-detached au-pair girl who is taking off most of her clothes and will shortly remove the rest as she is intending to take a bath. It is well known, a college lecturer once declared from a public platform, that men become insane through the study of au pair girls, and unless your answers have any value for him he will leap upon her, thoroughly jeopardise her, and exit, sobbing once more for the veil which has covered Druidism for centuries, into his dusky stationmaster's office.

But, but, but, they protest in Central Railway, Arrack Mines and all stations to the Hawkesbury, how can we reply to an advertisement that has no name and no address? Patience, patience, gentle readers! He is finishing it now, you must forgive him for his attention was distracted for a moment by an article in tomorrow's paper, of which he is an avid and conscientious reader. He intends to explain everything in the *Times* (good, good, he hears you ironically cheering) and will hasten to make available to you the full text of his advertisement as soon as it comes to hand. He has told us, through one of his aides, a Mr. H. Jacet, that as of now he finds repetitiousness appropriate to the situation as he evaluates it. He was not here, he said, merely to write an advertisement that would lift the veil that had covered Allen in Pitt Street, Central Railway and all stations to the Hawkesbury. In the world of today our three great nations, Pitt Street, Keflavik airport and Arrack Mines, must preserve at all costs their proud insular heritage which has been handed down to them as casually as possible by generations yet unborn. I come, he went on, to seize and bury her, not to praise her. The evil that au pair girls do lives after them, interred in the stones, weed-rocked, of Arrack Mines station, down platform, where the 5.45 p.m. from the city . . .

"For jesus sake!", Mr. Ecks interrupted, slamming down his glasses, "will you get on with the advertisement, man, and not be keeping us out of our beds! It's time, at last time to be going, and will you wind yourself up now like a decent man for the last of the farewell speeches we've been making to one another for the last three years and let us get away home to our nicer wives, nicer children and nicer au pair girls? Hey, Shenanagan, three more glasses!"

Meanwhile in Central Railway, Pitt Street and on the rocks at Dee Why they are awaiting, patiently, the full text of the communiqué. From as much of tomorrow's paper—the *Times*—as they have been able to piece together they have the following:

ANYONE possessing information on the life and writings of

but this, they complain, is not enough to go on. He wants a reply, doesn't he?, they justly observe, so he'll have to supply us with name, address and occupation: au delà de cette limite les annonces ne sont plus valables, comments Pierre Bernard, rédacteur en chef, from his dusky stationmaster's office. But he can't, he can't. He wants to run away, to renege, to go back to the boat, to a wet, slithery patch of slatted bench on the windward side to try for an easy take-off into suspended animation, hands on pullover inside raincoat through double pockets, ankles crossed as if chained, neck sunk into collar like broken metal soldier mended with matchstick. His last glimpse of the world always the coast of an island, each just like the other in the rain. And, as casually as possible, he admits it: he wants the replies now, before the advertisement is finished. He wants to hold back tomorrow.

6.

Hood, Mrs., and child. Horne, Mr. H. Hughes, Miss D. L. G. Hughes, Mrs. Hull, Mr. P. P. Humphrey, Mr. F. T. Humphrey, Mrs. and child. Hunter, Miss E. Hyde, Mr. E. J. Image, Mrs. M. M. Ironside, Lieut. J. G. Irving, H. G. Jacet, Miss H.

Orange Juice, Cream of Chicken, Fillet of Lemon Sole Galienni, Noisette of Lamb, Petit Pois, Wing Ribs of Beef, Potato cakes, Horseradish cream; Potatoes: Browned, Anglaise; cauliflower. Cold Buffet: Roast Leg of Pork, Strasbourg Duck; Salad: Lettuce, Radish; Dressing: American, French; Mixed Fruit Tart with Cream; Coupe Sans-Gêne, Apples, Oranges, Papaya, Pineapple; Ceylon Tea, Coffee—Chase & Sanborn. Coffee is also served in the Verandah Bar and Library.

This was the tomorrow she had been hoping for, the tomorrow that had only convinced her of its presence with the date on the menu, the name in the passenger list, and the copy of what was now today's paper lying there on her bed-table (the steward must have thought she wanted to keep it). It was a curious going-away gift, but then he was a curious man, not at all what she had expected at the beginning, but tied up in himself in a way that seemed to provoke in her not sympathy but irritation, a bad knot on a parcel one is trying to get undone. When he had handed her that paper, quite casually considering what their conversation had been up till then, and disappeared down the crowded stairs towards the entrance to B deck just when the loudspeaker had started growling All persons not travelling please proceed ashore, the tender is about to leave (though of course it was nearly another hour before they finally sailed) she wasn't sure what reply to make, and he was off before she had really recollected herself. Of course, perhaps that was his idea, to say goodbye as casually as possible, after all he hadn't really wanted to come out to the ship with her but agreed —perhaps to show how well he was known and respected after such a short time in the island, how long was it did he say? four years or thereabouts and scarcely a trace of an accent except for his funny way of saying YES like a police siren all runny and whiny. And the nice house he had, a family residence of character as El Inglés Simplificado might have put it, a home from home for a foreign girl and it might have been too if

Señorita Hermosilla Jacet finished adjusting her left earring, glanced in the full-length cabin mirror to make sure that nothing was out of place and decided to walk up on deck, or if not on deck at least as far as the verandah lounge, where they would probably be serving coffee— Chase & Sanborn—at eleven. She had missed breakfast without really intending to and it hadn't really been her fault that the steward had come back again without knocking and caught her in her nightdress (Mike? Spike?) so a little coffee would be more than welcome. She decided to take something to read, as much to repel any too pressing attentions (estos norteamericanos) as anything but also to fill in the time until lunch: Orange Juice, Cream of Chicken, Fillet of Lemon Sole Gallieni, Noisette of Horseradish, Mixed Ribs of Beef with Chase & Sanborn, Cauliflower Sans-Gêne, and her eye lit, by an extraordinary coincidence, on the copy of the *Times* (a local rag, he had called it, though she didn't at first understand this word) which he had handed to her, oh as casually as possible, looking rather (she repressed the thought) like a *mono*—how do they say that in Eengleesh?—with a bone or a plantain leaf. He wasn't much to look at, of course, those squat Amnesians rarely are, but his eyes when he ran them over you: vous me déshabillez des yeux as she once said to him in her bad French but he stiffened and grew pale—did he know too little bad French or perhaps too much? they certainly did things to you, even if the rest of him never quite lived up to the promise. Sometimes, indeed, he looked at her as if he were seeing someone quite different, and in bed sometimes muttered strange words mixed up with nonsense Spanish (which of course he spoke quite well): búsquelas en nuestras tiendas, things he might have read off a handbill. She decided anyway, after a moment or two of uncertainty, to take the *Times* up to the verandah bar with her. Big enough to hide behind, and at least she could keep up her English—Inish English (as he had explained to her) being a little different from the Gringo variety or even British English or the kind he himself spoke when perhaps a little drunk with his old friends (old bores!) down at Shenanagan's taverna. Making sure that she had her cabin key she made for the door but then on an impulse decided to make sure she hadn't her cabin key. Mike or Spike would probably be only too happy to let her in.

Going up the central companionway she misjudged the deck and found herself out on a level with the fresh air, though screened by the port fairing. The sea was grey, oily, uninteresting, but the waves seemed to notch, like some giant school ruler, the distance to Inish. The horizon swayed gently, the decks were moist like the outside of a cocktail shaker, the few fresh-air fiends wrapped in their blankets like dirty washing waiting for collection. She peered cautiously over the rail but a sudden sour smell from the engines began to mix unpleasantly with what was left of the hot-air-conditioning and she found herself a wet, slithery patch of slatted bench on the windward side, and closing her eyes, tried for an easy take-off into suspended animation, her ankles crossed to prevent the five inches of nylon becoming seven-and-a-half inches and

"A *Spanish* au pair girl?", interrupted Mr. Ecks. "Sure those ones never leave the apron strings. They'd be afraid of their lives to be alone in a house with a strange man, let alone a desirable residence".

"Mexicans", Allen replied dully, "are different. It's all a question of the C".

"And the proximity to the great USA", put in Shenana-

gan, who had been methodically polishing his glasses.
"You know—(he sang in a rusty movietone)—'South of
the borrrder . . . down Arrack Mines way!'."

"For jasusake", interrupted Mr. Ecks testily, "will you
let your man finish? . . .".

seven and a half inches and after her head had stopped
spinning and her tummy had quietened a little (it must be
just because I missed my breakfast: Noisette of Pineapple,
Browned Fruit Tart with Lettuce; Undressing: American
(Mike? Spike?) or French—because I'm naturally a good
sailor having travelled all the way from MAYA DE MEXICO
via Arrack Mines.

Señorita Jacet went along the deck and pushed open
the swing doors of the aft verandah lounge. Though it was
still fairly early, by shipboard standards, a number of
faces turned in her direction. Hood, Mrs. and child and
Horne, Mr. H. were reading the ship's bulletin. Hughes,
Miss D. L. G. and Hughes, Mrs. were knitting. Hull, Mr.
P. P. was impatiently waiting for the shutter of the bar
to go up. Humphrey, Mr. F. T. was not talking to Humphrey, Mrs. and child; Ironside, Lieut. J. G. was travelling
in mufti, and Irving, H. G. immediately looked at her legs
and then pretended he was expecting someone else.
Choosing a seat midway between the door and the bar
Señorita Jacet sat down, defying with a cold glance Irving
H. G. to look at her legs again and opened her copy of today's *Times* more or less at random:

> . . . has the chair heard the expression used three times
> by the Minister for Justice?
> Mr. Allen: I withdraw the word "lie"—it is untrue.

•

An Opposition Member: The allegation has been made and must be withdrawn.

Leas Ceann Comhairle: He has withdrawn it.

Mr. Ecks: What is the difference between a lie and an untruth?

Señorita Jacet quickly skipped the rest of the political column, and did not trouble to exercise her French on the daily snippet which today was headed LE POUVOIR DES DRUIDES SUR LES ELEMENTS (Ogham XI, 424) and didn't look very interesting. Instead, as is the habit with many women, she began at the back, skimming the births, marriages and deaths, alighting temporarily on the Houses for Sale columns (Attractive semi-detached family residence of character on bus route, convenient to shops, schools, churches. Accommodation comprises) and reverting finally to the personal column or Special Notices as they called it in the *Times* (these local rags!) where she was just about to read ANYONE possessing . . . when

"Excuse me", said Irving, H. G., stooping over her, swaying like one of those bottom-heavy toys with the movement of the ship, "but haven't we met somewhere before?"

"Please?" Señorita Jacet was at once at her most Mexican, me-no-speaka-da-language.

Irving, H. G. put his newly-acquired drink down on her table like a mountaineer siting a crampon. "Mind if I join you?"

Señorita Jacet buried herself once more in her paper. "Le druide ou le *file* est maître de l'eau comme du feu et l'on peut citer maints exemples de ce pouvoir. Celui-ci, entre autres . . .".

"You're not an Inishwoman? No, I didn't think so. Like myself, just there to see the sites, eh? Join me in a drink?"

Señorita Jacet's obvious embarrassment was being reflected in the activities of the other occupants of the verandah bar. Ironside, Lieut. J. G. had dropped several stitches, Hood, Mrs. and child and Horne, Mr. H., were in mufti, and Hull, Mr. P. P. was impatiently looking at her legs as if they were clad in seven and a half inches of the ship's bulletin. But Irving, H. G. was unperturbed.

"Say", he went on, unperturbed, "you going to Keflavik too? Thought I saw the label on your baggage last night as we came aboard. . . . I'm in the cabin next to you, number BL 4586 aft on D deck—now isn't that a coincidence . . .".

The ship gave a slight lurch which momentarily toppled Irving, H. G. back on his heels and played a little water-glass tune on the stemware in the bar. Hughes, Lieut. J. G. looked apprehensively at Hull, Mrs. P. P., who was apprehensively knitting. Both ladies pursued their lips and glanced apprehensively at Irving, H. G.

Señorita Jacet, by now thoroughly apprehensive, tried to bury herself in her *Times*. ". . . citer maints exemples de ce pouvoir. Celui-ci, entre autres, qui se trouve dans l'entrance porch and wide hall, large lounge, diningroom, four family bedrooms, bathroom, kitchen and pantry". Horne, Mrs. and child and Hood, Mr. H. were apprehensively reading the ship's timetable: 8.06 / 8.36 / 9.06 / 9.41 / 10.06 / 11.46 / 12EO6. Everyone in the verandah bar was waiting apprehensively for Irving, H. G. to turn into

but Señorita Jacet, with a toss of her raven head and a flick of her today's *Times* had risen from her chair, un-

avoidably exposing as she did so seven and a half inches
and had stalked out once more on to the deck.

"Arragh, that was a near one", said Shenanagan.
"Yes, indeed", said Mr. Ecks, wiping the perspiration
from his glasses and calling for a refill.
"Maybe you won't be as lucky the next time", said Allen.
"Maybe", said Mr. Ecks.

Señorita Jacet made her way forward, towards the Writing Room on the Main Deck. The wind tugged at the paper which she had whisked neatly under her right arm
and it was cold and raining. The decks for this reason
were almost deserted, silent but for the muffled revolu-
tions of the twin-screw turbines. The Writing Room, too,
was silent but for the muffled resolutions of writers screw-
ing themselves up to attend to overdue correspondence:
Parish, Mrs. Patrick, Parker, Miss S., Paterson, Mr. E.,
Penny, Miss C., Picard, Miss Mary, Pilkington, Mrs.
David. . . .

"Pilkington, Mrs. David?", interrupted Shenanagan.
"Ah now wait a minute".
"She married", said Mr. Ecks tonelessly, breathing
heavily on his glasses.

Pilkington, Mrs. David, née Allen, was having difficulty in
forming the first sentence of her first postcard. She glanced
up, absently chewing the top left-hand corner of her left
thumb-nail, as the door of the Writing Room opened, ad-
mitting a blast of Amnesic ocean and Señorita Jacet. She
smiled, thinking not of Miss Jacet but of something her
husband, Pilkington, Mr. David, had said to her last time

he wanted to make love to her, and Señorita Jacet smiled
back, thinking not of Pilkington, Mrs. David, but of Mike?
Spike?

"There you go again", interposed Shenanagan, drawing
a pint with the stub of an Inish-made Faber-Castell,
"nothing but sex. Several times recently I've read letters
in the newspapers on the question of modesty in dress,
mostly concerned with women's apparel and modern
fashions. You'll be quoting advertisements at us next".

Señorita Jacet came in, chose a seat at a table close to
the desk where Pilkington, Mrs. David was chewing the
top left-hand corner of her left thumb-nail, and sitting
down, once more opened her copy of today's *Times*, as
they call all these local rags.

Parish, Mrs. Patrick was reading the ship's bulletin.
Parker, Miss S. and Paterson, Mr. E. were knitting. Penny,
Miss C. and Picard, Miss Mary, were impatiently waiting
for their coffee to go down. They all turned apprehensive
eyes on Señorita Hermosilla Jacet.

"Comment mourut Loegaire le Victorieux?", she read.
"Ce n'est pas difficile. Aed Mac Ainine alla rejoindre Mu-
gain Aitinchairchech. C'était la femme de Concho-
bar . . .". And elsewhere she read:

Mr. Ecks: I received a petition from the defendant. I
received a Garda report and the comments of the trial
judge. On their merits I rejected the petition.

Mr. Allen: The Minister took action on the word of a
deputy of this House.

Mr. Ecks: I did not.

Leas Ceann Comhairle: This does not arise. The accommodation comprises: entrance lounge and wide porch,

large hall, and ANYONE possessing information on the life . . .

This, naturally, brought Señorita Jacet up with a jerk. She looked up to see Pilkington, Mrs. David's eyes keenly regarding her. She decided to speak.

"It is rough today, yes?"

Pilkington, Mrs. David decided to say nothing for the moment. She had, of course, recognised the young lady, recognised the nail-prints below the left shoulderblade, the teethmarks in unexpected places, the Mike? Spike? eyes which of course were only doppelganging. And since she, Pilkington, Mrs. David was the better concealed— three leaping years of marriage on top of the old nail-prints, teethmarks, and Pilkington, Mr. David (a far better doppleganger than Mike? or Spike?) she realised that the Señorita had not yet understood the precise nature of their encounter. So she straightened the postcard on the desk in front of her, momentarily tautened her stomach as the ship rolled, and began, for want of any other inspiration, with the address: Mr. Ecks, Arrack Mines Station . . .

"I knew it!", said Shenanagan, beamish with triumph. " 'Twas herself all the time! Sure well I remember the day the two of you were sitting here in this very bar—a rum and orange and a lager, if I'm not mistaken . . .".

"You are mistaken", objected Mr. Ecks, "that was no wife, that was my Mexican lady . . .".

"Gerrawayoudathat!", began Shenanagan, but Ecks was no longer listening.

Under the influence of the benificent heat of the Writing Room the clothes worn by Señorita Jacet and Pilkington, Mrs. David were slowly dissolving. This phenomenon was not, of course, observed by Parish, Mrs. Patrick, who was coughing into her knitting, nor by Parker, Miss S., and Paterson, Mr. E., who were travelling in mufti, nor by Penny, Miss C. and Picard, Miss Mary, who were still waiting for their coffee to go down. Señorita Jacet and Pilkington, Mrs. D., who were by this time all but naked, proved rather unambitiously to be not dissimilar, both having roughly the same protuberances, inclines and gradations, arranged in roughly the same way. But such is the contrariety of the feminine nature that in spite of discovering themselves wearing two similar bodies like two similar hats they immediately discovered something in common.

ANYONE possessing information on the life and writings of . . .

"Do you mind if I see your paper?"—Pilkington, Mrs. David smiled benignly at Señorita Jacet, who was nervously biting at the top left-hand corner of today's *Times*.

Señorita Hermosilla handed it over without comment. Pilkington, Mrs. David studied it for a moment. "You must call me Miss Allen", she said suddenly, folding it up and handing it back as casually as possible. "Are you having a good journey?"

"Comme ci, comme ça", replied Señorita Jacet, lapsing, for no reason that she could unconnect from Loegaire le Victorieux, into French.

"Well, dear, now that we're quite comfortable", said Pilkington, Mrs. David, shaking her flesh down round her like an ample peignoir, "we can have a nice cosy chat. Tell me, do you suffer from advertisements on the brain?"

•

I'm trying to introduce them as casually as possible, said Ecks into his rimless glass. I'm trying to get them to say to one another what they would never say to me, trying to unwrap each of them to vanishing point to see which disappears first, risking the knowledge of how much of me will go off with each of them. I'm trying to overhear them in a conversation that can only happen tomorrow, when they have read that advertisement in tomorrow's local rag, trying to see them in a nakedness of indifference, trying to cancel them out like plus and minus signs. . . .

"Try now", said Shenanagan, "try now and bring it up. You'll feel the better for it and I'll give you something to steady the stomach".

"It all started at a party", said Pilkington, Mrs. D., speaking quickly and not looking at all at Señorita Jacet or at Parker, Miss F. who was knitting, "somewhere on the North Shore between Dee Why, the Hawkesbury and Fassifern". She remembered:

Ecks: I do it for the money, I keep telling you. (He is lying on his back on the rocks at Dee Why or the Hawkesbury staring up at the stars, an almost-full bottle of Tooheys in his right hand. He is almost full.) Why else would one write pornography? The very committing to paper of private fantasies stops them being both private and fantastic, and the process becomes as much of a literary exercise as writing advertisements or attempting to lift the veil which has covered Druidism for centuries which, I may say, as an occupation I rate very little higher than inserting fake pornographic scenes into a noble work of English literature which shall be nameless, for example, *Pride and*

Prejudice. In fact one may go further and assert that the latter, as a contribution to the sum of human artistic activity, might indeed rate higher. Consider the problem of taking leave of Miss Bennet at the end of Chapter XXIV, following her stealthily to discover her in some long-drawn-out act of, shall we say, onanism, and tiptoeing back, style and composure unimpaired, to resume at Chapter XXV: "AFTER a week spent in professions of love and schemes of felicity, Mr. Collins was called from his aimiable Charlotte by the arrival of Saturday". But then perhaps it is because I learnt your language late in life that I have such a keen ear for its nuances. My pièce-de-resistance I consider the interpolation of a highly energetic rape scene into Thomas Love Peacock's *Headlong Hall*. The character of Miss Cephalis, though you recognise a suggestive assonance, is, you will admit, not the most immediately promising of material. . . .

"You no-hoper! You dill! You drongo!" Miss Allen turned on him a look of thorough contempt, giving her port, with the remaining full bottle of Tooheys, now warm, a vicious kick. "Drastic action is needed against a loathsome minority of New Australians who are shocking the rest of this community with their abysmal cruelty to dumb animals. But investigations reveal that the people who could deal out a much-needed lesson to these foreign sadists are failing miserably in their attempts to do so. Migrants caught in acts of cruelty are escaping all too often with paltry fines which do absolutely nothing to impress on them that Australians will not stand for such bestial acts".

Ecks (looking for the wrong stars in the wrong part of the heavens): I expect you say that to all your New Australian lovers. Look, why don't we go back to the party, and if you want to shoot through with that dill Pilkington I won't stand in your way. . . .

Miss Allen (getting up to go): That's that, then, and I can't say I'm sorry. So long, and have a nice life.

Ecks (detaining her by the ankle, looking up her skirt for the last time): It is my duty to warn you, Miss Allen, shortly to become Pilkington, Mrs. David, that in approximately ten years' time I shall be inserting an advertisement in a certain newspaper requesting that ANYONE possessing information on the life and writings of . . . I shall, of course, expect you to answer, giving as full as possible an account of your relationship with Mr. Ecks, not necessarily for publication, and including if possible original letters and documents, which will be carefully copied and returned. The advertiser will be particularly interested in any light that can be thrown upon Eck's emotional relationships with women, which never seem to have been completely satisfactory; and also upon his period in New South Wales, Australia, where he appears to have engaged in some kind of import-export business, worked for a publisher who specialised in rather expensive reprints of standard classics and begun, it is believed, his monumental thesis on Druidism in its Contemporary Manifestations, at which he worked for several months in the reading room of the Mitchell Library. It is hoped to devote a chapter to the parallels between his routine editing work, which he appeared to pursue very conscientiously (if one is to judge by the request slips from the Mitchell which have survived in his hand) and his more occult studies which, as you will know, remained unfinished at his

"I don't see that I can be of much help", said Pilkington, Mrs. David, with a sigh. "I don't see how I can answer this advertisement in today's *Times*. I mean it was ten years ago, I was young and foolish and . . .". Her voice tailed off ineffectually and Parker, Mrs. Patrick peered apprehensively out of her mufti. "I don't see that I can be of much help . . . but perhaps the two of us together . . . ?"

"Now, gentlemen", said Shenanagan, who had just been called to the bar, "now we'll see some action! The wife and the Other Woman! You wouldn't read about it! It was stated by the District Justice that he had taken the view that compliance with the Act did not require the last mouthful of drink to be taken simultaneously with the last mouthful of food, nor did it require that drinks be served to customers at the precise moment that food was served. If, at the end of a meal, a person ordered coffee and a liqueur and consumed the coffee first no offence was committed".

"Her name, as you have heard, was Pilkington", Mr. Ecks emphasised monotonously, "and therefore she was, or is, the wife of Pilkington, D. I very much doubt if the action that either you or I expect is going to materialise . . . now, if you will excuse me, I will return to my station".

"G'luck", said Shenanagan, turning the page to see if MAYA DE MEXICO had won tomorrow's big race.

I tried to hand it to them both as casually as possible, as if I were Parish, Miss S. waiting for my coffee to come up and eliciting feminine sympathy in the meantime. There was nothing wrong with the setting, give or take a few thousand tons. Ships are ships, even the Manly ferry:

•

the same lack of rules prevails, the same wave-rhythms in-
duce the same artificial pattern of excitement. We both, I
remember, had to run for it at Circular Quay—the last one
of the evening—and I almost gave her a little push because I could see the gap between the ferry wharf and
the boat widening and could almost imagine down there
in the harbour a shark's eye looking up her skirt. And
that was the trouble, of course, as she will tell me in her
reply in some altogether banal phrase several times recently I've read letters in the newspapers on the question
of modesty in dress

"I mean it wasn't even as if he was much good at it",
Pilkington, Mrs. D. pushed her permed head closer to that
of Señorita Jacet, who scratched her ear where some salt
spray had landed on her way from the clutches of Irving,
H. G., "but he just seemed to be thinking about it all the
time, if you know what I mean. I mean undoing the top of
my bathers when we were sunbaking without him want-
ing to . . . and then there was that job of his—the one
he used to do for that bludger down by Central Railway:
I mean sometimes you'd swear blind he hated it himself. . . .

Shenanagan yawned, obviously. "She's a bit of an old
gasbag, yer woman—wha' ?"

"Always was", assented Mr. Ecks out of the goodness
of his pint.

Miss Jacet, uncertain as to how to accept a confidence
from a non-positive stranger, wondered should she reply
in kind. Should she confess about that evening when semi-
detached in one of the four family bedrooms and bathroom? Or should she sit down at the next table, in be-

tween Paterson, Mr. E., who was still coughing, and Picard, Miss S., who was still waiting for her knitting to go down and try to write a reply to the advertisement she had not yet read in today's *Times*? She settled for the latter course, murmured a polite "Grand Evening" (the traditional Inish salutation as she understood it) to Pilkington, Mrs. D., who replied in traditional Spanish-Australian "Good Oña", and began looking carefully through the paper. Paterson, Mr. E., startled at seeing her looking through the paper at him, dropped a stitch and in bending down to retrieve it observed that the five inches of nylon had become seven and a half inches and

At this point the Writing Room door should open again. Enter, trippingly, from appropriate positions in the list: Draper, Mr. G., Draper, Mstr., Duncan, Mrs. F. and three children, Dwyer, Mr. W. T., Earp, Miss H., Easterbrook, Mrs. L., Ecks, Miss A. She strikes an attitude. Picard, Mr. S. gives a little scream and drops his knitting. Miss Hermosilla Jacet and Pilkington, Mrs. D. stare credulously at Paterson, Mr. E., as, still in his retrieving position, he prepares to

• ⸻

But meanwhile back at the station, Shenanagan was ruining the whole thing with those stage-Inish interruptions of his. But it wouldn't have worked anyway. I couldn't have relied upon Paterson, Mr. E. to sort it out amongst two of them, let alone three. "You have all three been brought together for a purpose", he would enunciate in his plain fashion, K3 tog. "Continue in patt., rib, cast off (care) and pull wool each other's eyes. Change to no. 7½ needles. Work in 11 rows (in Sydney, Keflavik,

MAYA DE MEXICO). Repeat patterson, rib, cast off (care) again and sew up. All three of you", and here he pauses to make sure that his needles contain lethal air-bubbles, "have agreed to reply to an enquiry, to be published in today's *Times*, addressed to ANYONE possessing information on the life and writings of . . .".

"Now if you will all make yourselves comfortable, if you will all turn towards the light so that I may recognise you clearly when you speak, we will proceed to analyse and correlate the information at our disposal. You, Pilkington, Mrs. D. have, I understand, claimed that the party in question was during the course of an Antipodean relationship importunate in the matter of sexual relations without being actually effective, and that you suspected him of a cerebral rather than a physical interest in the subject. I may shortly ask you to repeat your last two rows. You, Señorita Jacet, have, I believe, given evidence in another place and under another name as to the proclivities exhibited by the party in question when you had taken off most of your clothes and were shortly to remove the rest prior to taking a bath. To save you needless embarrassment we will permit you to change from 7½ back to 5 needles and p.s.s.o., but I reserve the right to suggest at a later stage that the fact that you conducted your liaison in bad French and in an attractive semi-detached family residence of character may have contributed to the degree of emotional frustration experienced by both parties in your attempts to pull the wool over each other's eyes. That brings us to you, Miss Ecks. I don't think that any of us are as yet aware of your precise role in this unhappy state of affairs. You come from a long line of Draper, Miss H., Draper, Mrs. L. and you therefore, one would presume, hold the most recent place, chronologically speaking, in the advertiser's affections. But we are not certain, and I am sure I speak for both Pilkington, Mrs. D. and Señorita Jacet, of what tension we are working to. Should we join shoulder, side and under sleeves seams against you as the one who has succeeded where we have failed? Are you in fact the only answer that the advertiser requires? Is he really interested in the information possessed by Pilkington, Mrs. D. and Señorita Jacet and, I might add in all modesty, myself? I have been patient with him and his Shenanagan. But I now ask myself, and your good selves, is it his genuine intention to have that advertisement published in today's *Times*, as they call all these local rags? Will he in fact try to hand it to you as casually as possible, with a grin and an underarm motion? Is he not, perhaps, content with his station, and making no more than a gesture towards lifting the veil that has covered Druidism for centuries? And if this is in fact the case, would it not be more prudent for us all to k1 p1 k1 p1 to the end and slide all stitches off needle? Materials: 5 to 7½ ounces Icelandic double-knit, a crisp-textured wool worked in a twisted stitch. . . .

● ————————————————————————

Meanwhile back at the station. . . .

● ————————————————————————

And moreover, ladies, there is another point to be borne in mind. If the advertiser is sincere in his request for information why, do you imagine, does he wait until we are all securely ensconced in the Writing Room of a liner upon the high seas or Amnesian ocean, outward bound from Inish, land of his adopted domicile, before publishing his request in today's *Times*—they call all these local rags the *Times*. I tried to put this to him as casually as possible but he gave me no satisfactory answer, referring me first of all to a Mr. Jacet who was at that moment greeting him with a nod of his umbrella and a wave of his head and was subsequently to be involved in some sordid romance with an au pair girl who had innocently entered his employment; and thereafter to a Mr. Allen of doubtful authenticity who represented himself as a professional Australian sensualist and also an even more dubious publican called Shenanagan whose only part in these sorry proceedings seems to be to cover up for the advertiser and /or Mr. Allen and/or Mr. Jacet and/or, of course, Mr. Ecks when one or another or all of them fails to find in the copy of today's *Times* which (sorry, they call all these local rags the *Times*) lies open before him at an advertisement beginning ANYONE in capitals possessing information on the life and writings of

● ──────────────────────────

Meanwhile back at the station. . . .

● ──────────────────────────

Now I put it to you ladies, and I see by the whiteness of your thighs that you are with me to this point—I put it to you at this juncture that the advertisement we have been asked to reply to in our several capacities is not, in fact, genuine. Not only, I suggest, will this advertisement fail to appear in today's *Times*astheycallalltheselocalrags, but the replies that it will elicit from your unsuspecting selves will in fact remain uncollected, unopened and unread. I am in a position to reveal that this advertisement is to appear, at the cost of an extra three words, under a box number. Is this not plain, purling evidence of intention to defraud? Does it not in fact suggest that the advertiser, far from seeking information on the life and writings of, is going out of his way, by an elaborate series of stratagems of which you, ladies, and myself are the unsuspecting victims, to avoid acquiring any information whatsoever upon the subject? It has already been made clear to us that his thesis on Druidism in its Contemporary Manifestations was, in fact, never completed, and that the only literary work standing to his credit, apart from the outline draft of an advertisement of doubtful intrinsic or extrinsic merit, is a series of new editions of popular classics which have found little favour in serious literary circles?

• ————————————————————————

MEANWHILE BACK AT THE STATION. . . .

• ————————————————————————

And, ladies, there is yet worse to come—and I can see by your 5 increasing to 7½ inches that you are all legs. Does not anything about this advertiser strike you as—well—suspicious? Do you not detect a certain similarity between this Mr. Ecks, a self-confessed Amnesian businessman living in a disused station in Arrack Mines, Mr. H. Jacet, a householder of doubtful morals residing in a nicer house with his nicer wife, nicer children and nicer au pair girl, and this Mr. Allen—not to mention Shenanagan, a publican of tedious manner and dubious authenticity? Now I put it to you, Pilkington, Mrs. D., Señorita Jacet, not to mention Miss Allen, that at one time or another one or another of these gentlemen has, on your own

•

admission, been admitted to your favours. But the question is . . . which?

With a muffled purl Paterson, Mr. E. subsided on the floor of the Writing Room, victim of his own ingenuity. The big ship was beginning to roll, knitting two and two together with every movement and, closing my eyes, I tried for an easy take-off into suspended animation, hands on pullover inside raincoat through double pockets, ankles crossed as if chained, neck sunk into collar like broken lead soldier mended with matchstick. My last glimpse of the world was the grey, distant shape of the Up platform, just like any other in the rain. I missed the five inches of nylon which coming down the footbridge (long since taken away) became seven and a half inches and

7.

Take stock again. On my left, MAYA-
DEMEXICOpittstreetsydneykeflavikairportpierrebernardanc-
ienrédacteurenchefandtomorrowstheycallalltheselocalrags-
the. On my right?

He moved cautiously in the chair. It was mahogany,
old-fashioned, circulating, one-time railway property,
grooved to the gestures of a forgotten stationmaster bending low to observe through the dusky window the Belpaire
firebox on the locomotive of the passing boat train. Stationmaster's office, guichet, waiting room, Writing Room
with black-bellied stove were now all one, the marks of
a new tenancy scarcely impinging upon their long-estab-
lished identity. Outside the narrow, dusky window the
Down platform was a mass of swineherd's fennel, piss-in-
the-air, smugwort, hickory and lesser anodyne, stirred by

a crepuscular wind into the simulation of an after-passion stomach: rippling, sweated with misty rain. The smugwort tugged at his feet as he walked down the Down platform towards where the section semaphore used to stand. They had forgotten to take away the tracks from the little siding and the avarice of long-dead Inishmen still wrung him: only one rusting cleat still held each chair to its sleeper. The wind sighed in a dusky treble in the telephone wires which still followed the path of the vanished tracks. He was at the end now, at the point where the ramp sloped off downwards in a Pythagorean demonstration to end abruptly against a cast-iron notice-board warning against trespass. Mr. H. Jacet would venture no further than the extremity of the pallisaded wooden station roof; Mr. Allen, obscured in a corner of the dusky first-class waiting room, would be pondering Bye-Law 45: Ceux-ci (les druides) prétendent qu'ils connaissent la grandeur et la forme de la terre du monde, les mouvements du ciel et des astres et ce que veulent les dieux; or number 46: No person shall wilfully, wantonly or maliciously move or set in motion any lift, engine or carriage or vehicle upon the railway or break, cut, scratch, tear, soil, deface or damage such lift, engine, carriage or vehicle or any of the fittings, furniture, decorations or equipment thereof, or any notice, number-plate, number, figure or letter therein or thereupon or remove any such article or thing therefrom or deface or damage any property (whether real or personal) belonging to the Board . . . which appeared to oppose flow against flux and guarantee that he would be, in a manner of speaking, alone.

He backed into the granite wall, into a gap where the descending creeper and ivy had formed a kind of niche,

offering him seven and a half inches of roof and the equiv-
alent depth of weedy, winnowy wall. He looked and listened. The treble wind. The dying whistle (Doppler effect) of the last boat train. The dying siren. The last mi-
cro-waves from the twin screws spending themselves
against the quayside. The last tram down Pitt Street:
green, sinuous, swaying. A sudden corner of a hitherto
unremembered road—where? Keflavik? Emain Macha?
Woolloomooloo? Every detail varnished and in place:
wearing traffic lines on the asphalt, a sagging wooden
fence, a dog with one ear up and the other down—a frag-
ment on the cutting-room floor of what is past or is to
come. Tout homme des Ulates qui ne venait pas à Emain
lors de la nuit de Samain perdait la raison: on dressait son
tumulus, sa tombe et sa pierre tombale le lendemain ma-
tin. A common experience, but it seems to happen more
frequently in this island: a sudden turn round the corner
into the memory of someone else's experience—a view of
your own trembling lips through the parted teeth of a girl
you are about to kiss, your own silhouette at a great distance against a Melanesian waterfall, the narrow circle
of light at the top of a waste-pipe wet with someone else's
vomit and tears. He looked towards the Up platform,
where he was just gallantly handing Señorita Hermosilla
and Pilkington, Mrs. D. into a first-class compartment of
the last train into the city, almost empty of course at this
time of year. He had chosen a first-class compartment, no
doubt, because he hoped to profit from the darkness without and the absence of corridor within to the extent of
amusing himself with, or perhaps even jeopardising, one
or both of the ladies. The door slammed with a wet, furry
reverberation. The locomotive, a 0-4-2 built in 1864 by

•

Sharp, Stewart & Co. with 17 in. by 24 in. cylinders and
4 ft. 9 in. coupled wheels, drew breath and purged him
with an exhalation. The red lamp glimmered to nothing
in the rain.

● ──────────────────────────────

Hic jacks. The splarges played quietly, as meditative as
the rustle of a turning tide. Messieurs, Fir, Caballeros, like
pubs they put a special seal on masculinity. The coin bal-
anced carefully between index and thumb (only one
chance) and dropped judiciously into the intricate mech-
anism produces nothing but an unseen feminine withdrawal. Then tabernacular whiteness and the musing
splarge-pipes, though in Inish there are no priestesses.
Here on Arrack Mines deserta, where the fountains for-
lorn no longer weep down on the pee, I am most likely to
encounter Mr. H. Jacet, Jack's the boy, the gentleman
whom we have left comfortably outside the window since
he didn't alight from the 5.45 p.m. from the city which
didn't stop, the one whose nicer wife and nicer children
and nicer au pair girl were more tantalising than most,
the one whose attractive semi-detached family residence
of character on bus route, convenient to shops, schools,
churches was worth far more than the very low ground
rent of £5-5-0 per annum, valuation £32. The auctioneers
recommend it as an easily-run, compact family, in good
structural order. No wonder Mr. H. Jacet remained on the
platform with a nod of his umbrella and a wave of his
head. And no wonder it is now necessary to seek him ten
metres up the Down to canvass his opinion on the likelihood of his replying to an advertisement in tomorrow's
Times beginning ANYONE possessing information on the
life and writings of

He ducked, stepping carefully through the puddles that had gathered at the entrance, and went inside. It took him some time to become accustomed to the bright lights after the gloom of the platform. Keeping close to the door he looked round carefully. The room seemed not to have changed. The pot plants were still green and growing, the midnight-blue nylon slip balled up in a corner, the two cigarette stubs still smoking in the ashtray, the radiogram still playing *Francesca da Rimini*. The view from the window was unchanged. The broad, golden expanse of Dee Why beach swept round to the ice-capped mass of Vatnajokull, and in the distance they were hammering up HERMOSILLO over a disused country railway station. He moved carefully over to the day-bed in the corner and lay down, removing his shoes and loosening his tie. On the radiogram a strangulated cadence slowly resolved; the cigarettes guttered and went out, leaving the raucous aroma of municipal rubbish-burning; and slowly a shape filled itself in on the narrow day-bed beside him, a female shape apparently fully dressed except for a midnight-blue slip. He rolled over, threw his timetable and umbrella savagely into a corner, and crushed her into his arms. As his mouth glued itself to hers his left hand moved stealthily upwards and groped at the fastenings of her handbag. In a moment it was open and he could feel the smooth silk inside. His other hand, descending avariciously, was tearing at the shoelaces of her stout brown brogues.

Then the world stood still.

It wasn't until they were lying in the dark fuming quietly that he spoke.

"Are you . . . ?"

"Of course", she replied, languidly pushing his hair

•   **74**

back out of her eyes. "But I shouldn't be speaking in
Inish—to you of all people. To you I am the nicer au pair
girl, the easy adventure, the baiser sur demande. Was I
worth the effort? Feel my extra smoothness (she caressed
the smooth, supple skin of her handbag); taste my extra
richness" (she titillated his parted lips with a long, slender
tongue that protruded from her sensible Inish brogue).
He folded the paper over in disgust but she would not be
suppressed. "Would you like to see how I look with four-
pence off? Would you like to take advantage of my free
offer?" But he was no longer listening. She was going to
tell him no more than all the rest; she was going to con-
found him with Mr. H. Jacet, to their mutual mortifica-
tion. The landscape outside had already changed. Nothing to be seen now but good greenhouse, fuel store, toilet
and garage. Nothing but a beautifully-kept garden enjoying quiet seclusion and, replacing the odour of detume-
scent Tchaikovsky, the evocative aroma of curmudgeon
cooked in its own juice, with a leaf of spandrel and a pinch
of rime.

Mr. Jacet hung his umbrella in the hall, stepping carefully over the rear portion of an articulated lorry manufactured in moulded poly-something which had been left
in his path, stopped by the cupboard under the stairs to
extract a bottle of sherry which he kept there out of harm's
way and carried it into his large lounge, depositing it
carefully on a mahogany-veneered occasional table before removing his walking shoes and assuming the faded
leather slippers with woolly insoles that had been laid out
for him. From the garden came the noise of children at
play, amongst which he could detect the accents of his
own son. It amused him not a little to detect the transfor-

mation of his own still distinctively Amnesian phonemes (in spite of Pitt Street, Keflavik and MAYA DE MEXICO) into the equally distinctive Inish accents of his son, and this within the space of only one generation. He had observed the same effect also in the speech of his nicer au pair girl who, though modestly keeping within the bounds of her native tongue when making love, could be heard upbraiding his son in virulent Inish idiom. Pouring himself a sherry he realised with a guilty start that he had been thinking these very thoughts in Inish, whereas he had promised himself a quiet half-hour of Amnesian life and culture each evening upon returning from his prospering import-export business to his nicer wife, nicer children and nicer au pair girl. One must resist—as he used to say to them down at Shenanagan's—one must resist complete cultural assimilation, if only for the sake of one's ancestors. And his friends would nod and look as if they believed he understood what he was saying.

He looked appreciatively round at his large lounge, through the large French windows of which he could glimpse his beautifully-kept garden that enjoyed quiet seclusion. He was proud of his large lounge, which was identical in almost every detail with those of his nicer neighbours to left and to right. He was proud of his beautifully-kept garden, which contained the same well-ordered array of choice hysteria, delicate clitoris and glowing hydrants as those of his neighbours to left and to right. He was proud of his nicer wife, who watched the same television programmes and then went out and bought the same packages as the nicer wives to right and to left. He was proud of his son, who was rapidly learning to scorn all things Amnesian and become more Inish

•

than the Inish. And he was ashamed of his nicer au pair girl because he was proud of the fact that he was ashamed to admit to his friends that he was proud of the fact that he had succeeded in establishing a liaison with her of a nature not stipulated in the contract and was frequently privileged to catch a glimpse of her removing the rest of her clothes before taking a bath.

Upstairs in one of the four family bedrooms was a neat filing cabinet containing in several well-ordered manilla folders the results of his detailed and painstaking researches into the subject of Druidism in its Contemporary Manifestations which had occupied him for many years and which was now almost reaching the point where he could anticipate contacting a publisher with a view to making the fruits of his labours available to the public at large. His reputation as a gentleman of serious purpose had been steadily increasing among his small circle of friends and his accounts of early pornographic experiences in the neighbourhood of Pitt Street, Sydney, were well received at the politer tea-parties which his nicer wife sometimes gave for some of their nicer neighbours. He was proud of his prosperous import-export business and of his growing circle of international contacts which included Pierre Bernard, ancien rédacteur en chef (1936-1946), MAYA DE MEXICO (Búsquelas en nuestras tiendas) and Jamsan Jokilaakson, J.J. to his friends. He was now reaching a point—and he felt that he could allow himself to say this without boasting—when he could foresee the day when he would be prepared to permit himself to indulge in something which had been dear to his heart these many years but which until now he had strenuously denied himself: the writing of an advertisement which would, he felt sure, prove itself worthy of acceptance for publication in the *Times,* a name which the leading Inish paper shared with many other "local rags"—as he understood the phrase to be. Not that he would approach this task in any spirit of levity. He was proposing to put forward a request to the effect that anyone possessing information on the life

At this point Mr. Jacet's soliloquy, which he had been conducting, in accordance with his resolution, in Amnesian—which translates rather pompously into Inish—was interrupted by the presence of his nicer wife, who appeared in the large lounge with a newspaper in her hands and a question, in Educated Inish, framed upon her lips.

"H", she said affectionately, buttoning his fly, "did you see this advertisement in tomorrow's *Times?*"

"I believe not, my dear". Mr. Jacet put his glasses carefully down upon the mahogany veneer, picked up, put on and adjusted his spectacles and directed his attention to the paragraph in question.

> The Inish Censorship Board (he read) has banned the following works on the grounds that they have been unusually and infrequently omniscient or epicene: Men Become Insane, by College Lecturer; Orange Juice, Cream of Chicken, Fillet of Lemon Sole by Hood, Mrs. and child; Station Sold, by Private Treaty; Druidism in its Contemporary Manifestations (for advocating the unnatural procurement of absorbtion . . .).

"Yes, my dear". He put the folded newspaper down on the veneered mahogany table. "I had seen it, but I don't think I shall apply. After all, we're getting a little old for that kind of thing".

•

He poured his nicer wife a little sherry and sat looking at her over the top of his glasses.

"I'm sure", he went on, "that plenty of people will come forward. It's not as if he hadn't any friends—a lot of the lads were very fond of him, and he was always the one for a good story . . . though I'm afraid not many of them could be repeated in mixed company, heh, heh. We must, I think, count ourselves privileged to have known him. Of course there was unhappiness in his life—I believe there was a woman in the case, indeed I've heard say perhaps several, but de mortuis . . . and then there was his scholarly work: he was just finishing a book, you know, when he left us—well, I'm sure someone in the proper quarters will see that it gets published, though it was a bit high falutin' if I understood it correctly. He was fond of you, too, you know; in fact he often asked me down at Shenanagan's, H, he'd say to me (he always called me H, it was his little joke)—H, he'd say, how's the mot? He was always trying to use what he called the *mot juste* but it sounded strange in his Amnesian accent. In fact I formed the impression that he was very anxious to *belong*, if you understand me, in spite of his queer ways. And his travels! Now there was a subject he could hold forth on four hours on end, though I must admit that when you'd heard once about his time in Pitt Street you'd heard it all. But sure he's gone now and

"I'd like some more sherry", said his nicer wife. "And would you ever see about that broken pane in the good greenhouse in the beautifully-kept garden?"

Mr. Jacet sighed as he took off his worn leather slippers and assumed his shoes. Marriage, he reflected as he passed through the bathroom, kitchen and pantry, was not all a bed of clitoris. But there was always the nicer au pair girl. And if he took his time over replacing the pane in the good greenhouse in the beautifully-kept garden he might even glimpse her taking off the rest of her clothes before taking a bath. . . .

• ────────────────────────────────

He wondered why the company had never come to take away the splarge and (as he hung his coat on the hook on the sweating door) why he himself had maintained the system in splarging order. It wasn't as if the stationmaster's old office, now the headquarters of a thriving import-export company, búsquelas en nuestras tiendas, was not equipped with all convenient modernisms. It was not as if he really enjoyed the walk down the deserted platform, particularly at this time of night when the rain lay puddled in the blunt furrows which once held sleepers and kennelwort grew lasciviously over the disjointed tie-rods of the long-abandoned signalling system. It was not as if this seat, innocent of varnish and with a one-centimetre crack where the two halves were coming apart, was more comfortable than any other, or the inscriptions, Protest Against the Judicial Murder of George Plant, Killjoy was Here, were any more absorbing than the old timetables which still lingered in the old stationmaster's old office. But as he sat there, his coat quivering like an expectant dog on the uncertain hook in front of him, he realised that this retreat could not be indefinitely sustained. Back in the office they would be waiting, determined to have it out, to answer the advertisement which each of them was carrying, as casually as possible, in a copy of tomorrow's *Times*. And he would sit there, looking out his dusky window at Dee Why, Keflavik, Pitt Street, Pierre Bernard, ancien rédacteur en chef, while they questioned him one after the other: why are you avoiding us? why are you separating us? why are you circumventing us? why are you circumventing yourself?

And he will turn to them with a plausible smile: "It's all in tomorrow's paper, ladies and gentlemen: it's all in the *Times*."

8. _____

"**B**UT it's not as simple as all that, surely?"
The walk back along the caulked planks of the platform
had been a slippery one. One after another the landmarks
fell away on the port bow—Keflavik airport, MAYA DE
MEXICO, Pitt Street, Pierre Bernard, all. When he pushed
open the door of what had once been the old stationmaster's old office and stepped into the fug only Z 3 was waiting for him, leafing quietly through his papers, brochures,
timetables, pocket surveys of Druidism in languages he
still believed he responded to more readily than Inish,
puffing on his pipe and scratching behind his ear with the
butt end of his glasses.

"I just dropped in", said Z 3, "in passing. Is it true you're
away? Really and truly?" But the sentence wasn't curled
up at the end in anticipation of a reply. Z 3 had known

he'd be off since the day he drove him up with his few possessions in the old car of which only one letter and one figure of the registration remained visible.

"I have no choice". Ecks spoke by rote, stacking and re-stacking his deskful of books and papers, the jetsam of his packing. "They let me export, they don't let me import—so (he exaggerated the Amnesian shrug even though Z 3 wasn't looking) how can I stay? Two years my last con-signment coming from MAYA DE MEXICO: I order March 29 two years ago—and when I get it? Half of them stolen by the Inish customs men. Have I all the papers? No, I haven't all the papers because MAYA DE MEXICO don't understand the tortuous Inish mind—you can't do the business, not the import-export business, that way". He pushed a jaunty quiff of strong chestnut hair away from his strong, chestnut eyebrow. "It's a pleasant island, I like it, your girls so charming, its mountains so blue, its la-treens, so purling—but when everything is going out and nothing is coming in . . .".

Z 3 had lit the gas-ring and was putting the kettle on for some unrevealed reason. There was no tea or coffee and all the cups had been given away or thrown out. "And what will become of this place?" He waved the stem of his pipe in a circular motion. "Ah, well I remember this line in its prime. The later 2-4-0 side-tank engines, built by the Company between 1892 and 1896, were Nos. 1, 6, 7 and 10, and had a more modern appearance than the en-gines of the early 'eighties. The coupled wheels had a di-ameter of 5 ft. 5 in. and the cylinders were 16 in. by 24 in. Two heavy six-wheels coupled goods engines, Nos. 50 and 51, were built by the Vulcan Foundry in 1891, with 5 ft. wheels and 18 in. by 26 in. cylinders. These were the only 0-6-0 engines on the line, until Nos. 17 and 36 were built at Grande Canaille Street works in 1899 and 1900 respectively. But the last-mentioned engines were not so large, the cylinders being only 17 in. by 24 in.".

The kettle was boiling now and he had picked up Ecks's last letter from MAYA DE MEXICO and was carefully steaming the stamp off. "For James", he explained needlessly (he had been doing the same thing for three years). "You'll send me a few now and again? No need to write— just pop them in an envelope".

Ecks considered the future. Somewhere waiting for him was another room, a hard chair that would receive the unfamiliar print of Inish tweed, a bare wall on which a picture or two, now in his trunks, would hang, a view: two sloping roofs, perhaps, the corner of a neon sign, a court-yard down below where at 9.45 every morning an old man would be reading a paper in another language, always stopping for approximately the same time at page eleven which contained the football results and page thirteen which listed the part-time jobs which he had not entirely given up hope of applying for, should he see anything that might suit him. Out in the street there would be an unpretentious café in which he would form the habit of taking his morning coffee, with a fat, rather surly propri-etress with whom he would slowly form a reluctant rela-tionship, perhaps on account of her daughter who was only sixteen but who already had a nice figure and a cer-tain way of looking. On his bed there would be a mattress, perhaps as yet unbought, or even unmade, which would assume the contours of his body and no other—for he would almost certainly sleep alone—and there would be a jacks the water of which would gush in a particular way.

•

Just waiting for the chemicals: the developer, the fixative, then the glazing machine which would after who knows how long give it a patina of permanence until one evening perhaps when the trunks would again be packed and some other Z 3, who would have arrived in the nick of time just as Mr. H. Jacet and Mr. Allen and Pilkington, Mrs. D. and Pierre Bernard, ancien druide . . . "Hrrr-mhp". Z 3 had coughed. "You'll remember now and again I hope, and a postcard for the lads if ever you get the chance—they'd appreciate it".

•————————————————————

He had begun to dream of his Amnesian childhood. Boys with names in what now seemed an impossibly foreign language spoke to him with the familiar pronoun about games, the rules of which he had long forgotten. He recognised them, reluctantly, but the scenery had changed. The village station, with a low platform of course in the Amnesian manner, was consigned to a corner of Sydney Central, which in its turn was confined somehow within the twin limbs of trackless Arrack Mines . . . and there seemed no way of cleaning off the imposed images. Then the boys became men and moved, took on new nationalities, spoke new tongues, most of them a kind of Australian-Inish that was both unlovely and unreal. But beneath the false moustaches, the advancing hairlines, the differently-shaped paunches, the differently-paced prejudices, there was a confusing similarity, a concatenation of echoes so that now when he looked over at Z 3

•————————————————————

". . . that time in Sydney", Z 3 was saying, so that for a moment Ecks was neither here nor there—"you never did finish telling that story. You remember the time when you had that job . . .".

Mr. H. Jacet gestured primly, libidinously from the shadows by the ticket-wall.

"There was nothing to tell, really", Ecks said hastily: "It didn't last for very long. The police or somebody were getting suspicious. I didn't wait to be asked any questions".

"And you'll be asked no questions this time either".

After a moment's thought he decided that Z 3's remark was meaningless, and intended to be. They sat in silence for a while, listening to the drip of the rain somewhere out on the platform, the last of the coal crackling in the stove, Ecks staring hard at a steely-blue patch on the top of the old stationmaster's old desk where ink had been spilt very long ago.

Z 3 he had classified on first acquaintance as the typical Inishman and he had never moved him from that category since. Z 3 had classified him on first acquaintance as the typical foreigner, and had never moved him from that category since. The warmth of their friendship was thus retaining its lukewarm constancy to the end. They had discovered, fortunately at the same moment, that there was sufficient heat in the affair to sustain the occasional telling of jokes—a field in which neither of them excelled—but inadequate thermal capacity to withstand a serious conversation about personal relationships. So since neither knew anything about the other they felt safe and comfortable when together and thought their own thoughts: the one in Inish; the other, as often as not, in Amnesian.

"You were going to put in an advertisement"—Z 3 was filling his pipe—"for someone to take over the goodwill. Did you hear anything from it at all?"

"I changed my mind. The goodwill seems to have evaporated together with the last of the stock. I thought it better to cut my losses".

Though of course he had actually made money: not a great deal, but enough to start again in that as yet undeveloped, unfixed and unprinted room with some girl typing for him who was perhaps even now combing out her hair after washing it and reading the advertisement columns of the paper in which his advertisement of a vacancy, cautiously worded, would soon appear, their two lives approaching one another inescapably. He would interview them himself, of course, enjoying the pretty ones, looking out of force of habit at their legs but selecting the plainer one who seemed to need the job, the one who would turn out to be only partially efficient, not bad enough to sack, the one towards whom he would feel absolutely nothing emotionally until one night he would dream of her but with the voice and mannerisms of some childhood and forgotten love and the next day everything would have changed and he would stand closer to her when leafing through the morning mail MAYA DE MEX and something would happen or nothing would happen.

"Nothing would have come of it anyway", continued Z 3. "Sure most of that crowd wouldn't recognise an opportunity if it came up and shat on them. Though I knew a feller once sold a piano in three days through an advertisement. Riddled with woodworm too. But then there's one born every minute".

The birth of a woodworm is perhaps, yes, an important

event—being celebrated no doubt this very minute in the leg of the chair in that unlocated office in that as yet unknown building in that as yet unknown country . . . New York and then south, perhaps—not Mexico en nuestras tiendas la bellísima Señorita H. but further Santiago de Chile, Concepción, Chacabuco, Señor Ecks, *Intendente Mercantil* and a brand-new Z 3 in South American Spanish with hissing, splarging Cs:

"Buenas noches, Señor Zeta Tres".

"What was that?" But he was not really curious, probably only half-heard.

"I was just trying you out in Spanish. Like to come into partnership? For a modest investment?"

Z 3 smiled because he knew it was not a joke. Like all untravelled Inishmen he knew a lot about the world.

"I don't see meself in foreign parts. There isn't a place you'd get a decent pint".

A stable horizon, a positional sense of birth, marriage, death, a cause, a *patrie*, a comfortable insularity. You can't grow it, grow into it, you must learn to live without it, or live outside it, or get out. "If you ever go across the seas to Pitt Street . . .".

"Z 3", he said, "did you ever wonder what brought me to your island?"

Z 3 was too old a hand to be taken in by that one. The traveller who expects the natives to ask him questions rather than the other way round must be an uncertain commodity even to himself. And all those who came to Inish, he knew from folk-experience and lachrymose hearsay, were for ever explaining themselves to those who had no inclination to listen. Instead he got up and inspected the cupboard in the corner, in which in the olden

days the spare guard's flag used to be kept. He found a
tin of sardines.

Ecks recognised the tin. It had been there when he had
moved in, four years ago next March 29th, and even then
it had lost its paper wrapping and someone, presumably
in trying to open it, had broken off the little metal tongue.
He had cut himself on it almost without noticing.

"Would you look at that!" Z 3 held up a bloodied finger.
"I was going to say it would make a kind of a last supper,
if you'll pardon the illusion" (he always talked in this
stilted manner when he hadn't anything to say), "but perhaps it would be wiser to dispense with ceremony. Will
you come down the road for a jar?"

"No", replied Ecks, "I haven't finished my packing".

They looked away from one another in silence for a
while, Z 3 presumably waiting for the exemplification that
would round out the previous proposition and give him an
excuse to leave—or rather not to stay, since he seemed determined to dissolve into absence and so avoid a positive
leave-taking.

"Are they seeing you off on the boat?"

Both of them knew that there could be no *they* that was
not included within these three walls and a similar three
walls—or two, leaving out the bar—of Shenanagan's pub
where even now Mr. H. Jac. . . . and all other, dimmer
theys: Herr Doctor Smith or Kleinmaus with a beard or
was it a moustache that he talked to once for five seconds
about the thorny question of prime numbers or was it
tanged adzes in Fassifern or was it Toronto, New South
Wales on a sunny winter's day in February; or a schoolboy
with a fat face and a leer who sat on his head (hot, dirty
flannel) and threatened to castrate him with a pair of scis-

sors—the name on the blades Krokodil but the name of the boy? Or an adolescent female, where, whose eyes looked as if she was being raped but who was in fact reading a story about a pet rabbit, he saw it over her shoulder, but in what language? Or several military theys with mercifully scrubbed-out faces but all more dusky than Mr. H. Jacet greeting him with a nod of his umbrella and a wave of

". . . off on the boat?"

"No".

"You'll be on your own, so".

"Yes".

"Well, if you can lend a hand with the traps at all . . .".

How many between here and there. Outside the door, trap number one, a view. Let's Go Out Today. Sunday's walk in South Arrack Mines is recommended for antiquarians, blackberry gatherers and ghouls. The ruins of Rathjacet church date from the twenty-ninth century. The most interesting feature there is a collection of ancient timetables which are now fixed to the walls. They are ornamented with simple designs and while there is no doubt they are many centuries old . . .

". . . ding the paper?"

"Just something that caught my eye". Ecks unostentatiously folded the paper again. "You were saying?"

"If I can lend you a hand with the traps . . . ?"

Number two, attractive semi-detached residence of character. Number three . . .

". . . o'clock, did you say?" Z 3 was still laboriously making a scaffolding for a conversation. "That'll give you plenty of time for a pint in Shenanagan's before the boat

•

train. You wouldn't have such a thing as a corkscrew left
in the place, I suppose? If you have I'll drink your health
in sardine oil".

Ecks thought of telling him that there was one in the
recess at the back of the waiting room on the Up platform,
then thought he might be quite unsettled if by any chance
he found it to be true. The point was broken off it anyway. So he retorted simply by raising one thick, strong,
jaunty eyebrow at Z 3's back—he was pointing towards
the single bulb trying to discern a weak place in the tin—
a retort which the latter pointedly ignored.

"D'ya know I could never master one of these things".
Z 3 enunciated with emphasis as if suspecting the presence
of non-Inish-speaking sardines; "You know the way it
never rolls straight but deviates on a magnetic course instead of pointing true north. And you're left with no more
than half the interior delights exposed—almost indecently
provoking apart from the fact that when you've dug them
out they're nothing but ectoplasm. But then I suppose
you'll be eating them fresh where you're off to".

He would naturally imagine that I am seeking the sun,
running south under full sail, or at least west, the direction of opportunity.

"Or is it back to Australia you're going? Sure you might
as well once you start . . .".

Both of them were becoming weary of this unspoken
antiphon, Z 3 with having to leave the necessary gaps for
Ecks's thoughts, Ecks with having to fill them with something suitable to the occasion. I have thought, he thought,
my last word on the pangs of upheaval, my last word on
the mysteries and complexities of the land of image, the
last prurient image I shall ever indulge in this station.

"I have spoken", spoke Z 3, "the last word I shall ever speak in this station on the remarkable class of 0-6-2 tank engines built by Kitson and Co. in 1897. Cylinders 18½ inches by 26 inches. Coupled wheels 4 feet 9 inches. Found unsuitable in original form and altered to 0-6-0 tender engines in 1908".

They were of course wrong—both of them—but it gave them an excuse for action, and excuse to stop sitting there and not looking at one another. Z 3 went over to the platform side of the room and began banging the sardine tin cautiously against the defunct gas-bracket.

"If we could only let the air in and destroy the vacuum we could prise it up with a knife or something. You wouldn't have a knife left in the place I suppose?"

Ecks looked carefully through his pile of books and papers, half-closing his eyes to prevent a word from creeping up on him unawares. How much longer would Z 3 stay? He had known him remain till two or three in the morning, drinking cup after cup of instant coffee (though usually he took nothing but strong tea) and reading through the old timetables in which there still breathed for him the forgotten wheel-arrangements of the 0-6-2Ts. But now there was no coffee, no arrangements and

"There is no knife".

"Ah". Z 3 stopped banging the tin, which had been thudding fuzzily against the cast-iron as if it were packed with disposed-of napkins and peered at it in the hopes of detecting a tell-tale bubble of sardine oil. The inspection revealed nothing.

"We'll call it a day, so. And if you won't be coming down the road . . .".

•

"I don't think so, thanks. I've still one or two things to do and . . .".

"Ah sure I know how it is. Well lookit, come down if you can. And if not . . .".

"But I'll see you a piece of the way". The idiom was not quite appropriate to urban Inish but Z 3, lost in a cloud of old steam memories, did not for once remark upon it. They went out of the old stationmaster's old office through the door leading on to the Down platform, down the Down platform and down the ramp leading down at the end of the Down platform and on to the road, which Z 3, being an old steam man, always called the grassy avenue, still barred as if a very long ladder had lain upon it, the last impression of the railway tracks which had once shuddered under the sextuple driving wheels of 0-6-0 no. 17, built at Grande Canaille Street in 1899, cylinders 17 in. by 24 in., wheels 5 ft. 0 in., withdrawn in 1929. They walked together for perhaps fifty metres until the hedges and gates and walls on either side of the road began to offer unmistakeable signs of encroachment. The urbanities of the nicer suburb had begun to nibble at the old right of permanent way, Trespassers Prosecuted. It was at this point that Z 3 always became embarrassed, almost shame-faced over the state of his road and Ecks judged it tactful to leave him. They stopped at a point where an elegantly swelling and reversing curve in the grass indicated an erstwhile crossover.

"Good crossing now. And you'll send the odd card?" The handshake, the first and last in their acquaintance, made a poor connection and no spark jumped the gap.

"Goodbye. I'll be back one of these days to see how you're all getting on". The trite response, Ecks thought, would have sounded even triter if he had attempted to answer the question. He turned on his heel and back again. But Z 3 had already and not unsurprisingly vanished.

The wind had freshened, blowing straight down the tracks from the distant city, carrying the smell of malted granite, of rich gutter water, of stale shoulder-straps in sodden buses. It carried also, from beyond the terminus, scampi on the rocks Dee Why, Orange Juice, Cream of Chicken, Fillet of Horseradish Gallieni, Mixed ribs of Chase and Sanborn . . . there was even a hint of Iced Lava in it when he arrived back between his two platforms and found her sitting on the cold stone edge on the up side, swinging her elegant five inches of nylon, which because of the wind became seven and a half inches and

"Another of your useless friendships? Who was he this time? A plumber? Or just another peasant?", she P'd vigorously over him, Australian triphthongs trailing round her like Doppler-effects. He shrugged, pointed the way to the door on the down platform, pointedly looking up her skirt as she got to her feet, pointedly got to her feet as she was about to try to jump from the platform to the road, gripped her round the thighs, feeling the skirt slither on the slip, the slip slip on the pants, the pants as he sought to release a suspender, to suspend her once more in triumph before lowering her to the laddered grass under the thundering wheels of 0-6-0 no. 17, built at Grande Canaille Street in 1899, withdrawn in thirty seconds flat!

"You were quick". It was neither a compliment nor a protest.

"Too quick". It was neither a question nor a statement.

"No". It was neither an affirmation nor a denial.

•

She was still breathing heavily.

"Your pants are very short".

"That's the latest fashion, you dill".

"All the easier to . . .".

They were back in the old stationmaster's old office, sharing the tin of sardines. "You were the last one I expected. I thought, after a bad time just a little while ago, I was managing rather well. Z 3, you know, is a man of honour, minds his own business, never asks questions, never expects answers, never comes from anywhere, never goes anywhere . . .".

"Z 3?"

"It's an ancient order among Inishmen. Difficult to get into—you have to have the right connections, the right wheel-arrangement. I remember him telling me of a 2-2-2T no. 21, built at Grande Canaille Street in 1873 . . . but no, I wasn't expecting you at all. In fact I was just about to write you an advertisement—you may have seen it, in tomorrow's *Times* in fact . . . yes, there's a copy on my desk on top of Daniel's *Philosophy of Ancient* . . . well it *was* there I'm sure, surely I couldn't have packed it . . .".

She wasn't listening. "Well, you certainly were expecting someone. Or do you always go around wearing one now? They're illegal in this country you know, classified as usually or frequently indecent or obscene. You always were a bludger and you still are. I must have been shickkered when I married you".

"But I can explain it all quite simply, m'love. You see this girl was far from home and in a strange land and naturally being a stranger here myself I felt that the least I could do was to catch a glimpse of her removing the rest of her clothes before taking a bath. I can insure you . . .".

"For how much?" The sharp-tuned phonemes cut like an auger flighter. "I never got a penny out of you, much less anything to remember you by. Except . . .".

"Yes?" He could see the epigraph:

> I never had the good fortune to know my celebrated father, as he had left Australia before my birth, and circumstances—which I need not go into here—kept us apart until his . . . I count it, however, an honour and a privilege as well as a filial duty to contribute this introduction to a work which future generations will not only consider as a masterpiece in its own right but as a monument to the genius

". . . but of course I got rid of *that* in good time". She extracted the last, foetid sardine with the blunt end of a match. "So really I don't know why I came all the way from Dee Why". At least no son of his would flaunt such a semi-vowel. "Except to tell you to forget about that advertisement—it isn't going to make a bloody bit of difference".

"Ah but it is". Proud of his long initial Inish A, he drew it out a little, listening for a harmonic from the now-empty sardine tin. Ah, ah, aaaaah . . . finally it responded, in the region of a high A natural. "You see, my dear, it has already made a difference: finality is all. When you reappeared so conveniently on the cold stone on the Up side, cold stone on the backside, you were no doubt intending to prolong your stay. But you are powerless against my decision: see—you are thin, sparse, evanescent. Through you I can already read Only Best Drinks Stocked J. J. Shenanagan March 1948 1 2 3 4 5 6 7 8 9 10 11 12 13 14 15 16 17 18 19 20 21 22 23 24 25 26 27

•

28 29. Your fingers have met one another in the middle of that sardine tin, your triphthongs are indistinguishable from the ardent whistle of 0-6-0 no. 17, built at Grande Canaille Street in 1899, withdrawn in 1929. I have put words between us, more potent than distance, more lasting than promises, more real than finger-ends. You would never have answered that advertisement except under a pseudonym, and the *Times* will not take responsibility . . .".

The hand holding the sardine tin faltered, rematerialised.

"I forgot to mention", Z 3 added, "that the young lad does be collecting them things. He makes tanks outa them".

"How many does he need for a tank?"

"Only the one. He puts pinkeens in them—one fish, one tank, modern living conditions. They're dead by the morning but I feck them out and tell him the cat got them. Trouble is he is always on at me to get a new tin. Says they get radioactive—would you believe that? Now if you'll excuse me I'll wait a bit until the express goes down. You'd never hear it behind you on a night like this until it was too late. You've objection if I eat this last sardine? Put it out of its misery?"

"Help yourself".

She ate it in one gulp.

"Break it down, Joe—here I am and here I stay. Not for the second time you don't. And after what just happened—well, I mean you never know, and then I'd really be in strife". She walked slowly round the old stationmaster's old office, stickybeaking.

Ecks decided to let her have her stay. It seemed the only thing to do.

9.

It was the untypical details that came up first. Under the house, with the bicycles, antipodean handlebars crooked upwards, were a number of domestic objects, their precise outlines now forgotten, which keyed the evening. They spoke of family, of the overspill of domestic bric-à-brac that a man living on his own never accumulated, of a casualness about nails and dead men and old newspapers which a bachelor can only affect. To meet these objects at night was worse: they lived their own relentlessly useless lives even more intensely, proclaiming the somnolent, cluttered ease of existence behind an emotional palisade where there is more than one tamed mutineer. There was even a bottle, Tooheys Flag Ale, not quite empty, whereas he would have made a point either of finishing it, or of washing it, or of leaving it somewhere where his planned insouciance would have been noticed. He crouched down under the house, waited for the objects (the old motor tyre, the empty tea-chests, the perfunctory gardening tools) to take him over, make him one of them; while outside in the moonlight his head was swimming away on its own and above him, through the thin floor and the fibro, the radiogram and the feet seemed to be nailing up a door from the inside.

It was a party like many others. A few strangers and he managed to float peacefully by them on three or four carefully chosen anecdotes of a Europe he felt he had just invented before the drink made him careless of his antecedents and conscious of his isolation. This didn't happen with tragic regularity at every party—that would have been bearable: but just once in a way, even perhaps when he was a link in a charmed circle of rhetoric or a positive pole vigorously emanating towards some female negative, he heard the doors closing with a rubberised thud behind him, saw the tail lamps of trains threading across the points at the platform end, watched the ship-to-shore streamers breaking, heard the silence in a room in which everyone had deliberately stopped talking. One recourse was tears—old-fashioned Amnesian tears—but this was extreme and frequently impracticable. The other was to go on, to the next drink or the bed or the grass outside, where the party-noises ebbed and flowed like shell-shocks and the Southern Cross burnt crookedly above. This time, however, it was swimming: everyone had suddenly decided to go down to the shark-proof pool (it was a very hot February night and the humidity hung like fungus). Three of them, to prove that New Australians couldn't swim,

threw or pushed him in: that was the first thing he remembered after the gardening tools.

The next was back in the living room. It was so hot they
were all still in their bathers, and his were old and slack
so that if he was careless about the way he sat they became stupidly indecent. One girl had made an elaborate
pantomime of rolling the top of her suit down to dry herself under a towel, and seemed disappointed that no one
was taking more notice: in fact only the host was paying
attention and he was watching her avidly in a mirror, being watched equally avidly by his wife, being watched
equally avidly by a Holden car salesman who had been
around a lot lately, being watched by the girl with the
rolled-down bathers, being watched now, through some
kind of centripetal attraction, by Ecks.

There was one man outside the circle. Ecks did not remember having seen him before the swim—he must have
arrived when he was under the house with the still life. He
was a craggy individual, pea-wrinkled in the Australian
manner, with an outback drawl that may or may not have
been affected. He had cornered a bottle of Woodley's Est
and was steadily absorbing it, proclaiming all the time
that it was too bloody warm.

The towel-girl had contrived to slip into her bra and
was pulling her dress over her head. Conversation free-
wheeled as everyone waited for her to try to get out of the
rest of her bathers and put on her pants. But she folded
up the towel, made it into a cushion and sat on it. Faces
went blank.

"Hey, Col—", the Host groped around for a subject.
"You've never seen this bunch of jokers before—what do
you make of them?"

•

The Estman looked round the stony-eyed circle, druidically irregular. It now became apparent that he had indeed only just arrived—though by now it was at least 2 a.m.—and that he was a stranger to everyone but Host. Even Mrs. Host was looking at him as if he might pour himself, genie-like, into the Est bottle and pull the cork in after him.

"Go on mate", somebody probably said. "Give us your candid opinion".

"Fair dinkum?" Estman seemed no more than mildly interested.

"Go on, be the fortune-teller. What the wino foretells. Truth in the bottom of a plonk glass". The mild insults seemed not to register.

"Give it a go, Col". Host was determined to try anything rather than think of the mermaid towel-girl waiting to be untailed. "Start with me if you like . . .".

Estman gave him a look close to contempt. "Fair go", he drawled, "you and me are cobbers. Now this joker here . . .".

He turned to the Holden salesman, a pink-faced, slick-haired individual, and blinked at him over the top of his glass. "Age? You're younger than you look, I'd say. I wouldn't put you at more than 28, though you look a good 35, every bloody day of it".

Holden's grin wobbled. "Not bad guessing—29 next month".

"I'd say you're in business too—something sedentary", his accentuation of the second syllable made it sound like an insult. "The rag trade?"

"No, you're way out on that one". Holden's tone was firmer, though he and Mrs. Host were painfully not looking at one another. "You could say I was in business though, alright".

Est grunted, apparently lost interest, and turned his attention to the bottle. Somewhere over on the main line towards Fassifern an engine hooted. Holden's business no longer seemed to be of any importance. Someone put on a record, since the towel-girl still showed no signs of moving, and Mrs. Host opened a tin of sardines.

"And that's where you made your big mistake", she said, prodding around in the oily tin with a broken nail. "If you hadn't been so bloody interested in whether or not I was going to get out of those bathers we wouldn't be here today. Or rather—", she glanced round the old stationmaster's old office with distaste, "you wouldn't. Anyone can see that this is the end of the line".

He had made that watered remark to Z 3 the second night of his tenancy, four years ago next March 29th, next March being a leap year, when he was still trying to handle everything as casually as possible but still had to relearn for the xth time not to make jokes in other people's languages. In Australia it was all right because everything you said was taken seriously particularly if you spoke with a New Australian accent but here in Inish he had yet to get used to the technique of ageing a joke by repeated exposure until it concentrates and becomes part of living idiom; anyway Z 3 had said nothing, assuming that any comment would have been taken as referring to the substance rather than the shadow, i.e. that an agreement might cast doubts upon his, Eck's, business probity and ability whereas a disagreement, on the other hand, would have suggested that he, Z 3, had not found the joke funny and the only safe solution was silence. So he had fiddled

•

with that old knife he had carried trying to straighten a valanced flange on the gas-bracket that had got knocked as he said baw-ways or bocketty when they must have been moving out the big ticket rack which he had hoped they might have left for he could have filed in it his many fragments f.o.b., c.i.f., e. & o.e. MAYA DE MEXICO invoices in sextuplicate for the benefit of the Customs and Excise and even then it was pinched on him the same as in Australia when all he had was a few innocuous souvenirs from the old country for research he had said but they had smiled rudely yes of course mate and taken them away.

"Whatever happened to old Ecks?" said the man with a wog in his beer.

"Oh he had this book of his, yer see, but he gave it away . . .".

But by then he could translate, and so shrunk instead behind Pierre Keflavik at BL 4586 and pretended he hadn't heard.

She had finished the sardine tin, the remains of the oil now having been transferred from the metal via her fingers to her lips, and, standing up, began to unwind the towel, wobbling like a decellerating gyroscope. She was, of course, fully dressed underneath, but if she had hoped for any effect she must have been disappointed, as Estman was firing again on all cylinders (I always had trouble with mechanical metaphors), this time in the direction of Mrs. Host.

The words by this time didn't matter. Everyone was full, and at that point of fatigue when the careful enunciation of any word or group of words will load it or them with a rocking pile of meaning which everyone stands round with baited breath hoping to catch. Estman spoke slowly in any case, but when shikkered his enunciation barely sustained the necessary elisions and terminal unvoicings. What Ecks thought he was saying was that Mrs. Host was the right wife married to the wrong man, and then of course he had the two of them, looking left and right but watching one another in the mirror, whilst Holden, clearly wishing he was miles away and had never come within fondling distance of Mrs. Host's available charms, was getting a completely different message that spelt this is the end of the carefree feeling of pushover and the beginning of something that is going to be long and repetitive and uncalculable in terms of percentage. Ecks in his turn was reading it at that time as a frieze of voices, grunts, glass-clinks, skin stretches, heat-itches, mosquito taps against the screen doors, nothing more, since his track had suddenly switched him back into Amnesian and the language around him was as foreign as that of a druidic rite. It was at this point that he noticed that the towel-girl was making the awaited change from bathers to pants (the all-dressed look had been a protective illusion), not being too careful but not displaying either, acting as if she were alone with herself but being decorous out of habit. She saw that Ecks saw, and he saw that she saw that he saw, and perhaps because he was thinking in Amnesian the lasciviousness of which does not read clearly in the face she saw that he saw no more than a nice girl exchanging bathers for pants and not je lui avais même déboutonné sa robe par derrière and smiled while hoisting them or it into position a friendly you're a nice safe man smile and we're well out of this together whilst Host and Mrs. Host and Holden are being walled up in their triangle by Estman.

•

But at that moment Estman misfired again, his motor died with a rumble (are these mechanical images precise enough?) and he began groping around for another bottle. "There's a cold one outside, Coll", Host had said, hating to have to send him away and leave the triangle without its dropped perpendicular but that's the way it had happened and Ecks was left connected up to Towelgirl by the wrong wiring, parallel when it should have been series, and before anything could be done "Put on another record" said Mrs. Host to no one in particular, giving Holden's hand a surreptitious goodbye-for-ever pat which infuriated him, you could see, for two reasons at once; and then Estman was back, talking a blue streak as he came through the door—he must have opened the back screen-door for air or something as he was followed by a stream of bugs and wogs and beetles like a self-powered halo.

"I've got *your* number though, mate". He was talking to Ecks. "The European mystery man. How long you been here?" He named the exact time. "Where do you come from?" He named a country not a thousand kilometres from Amnesia. "And you've come down in the world, haven't you? Or you think you have. The bloody Aussies won't let you practise your noble profession so you're reduced to the ranks of a humble sanitary carter, eh?"

These weren't the words, but they run close enough to the meaning. Estman was building up his other triangle (I don't think I can carry this metaphor much further), laying a foundation of benevolent abuse so that he could draw in Towelgirl and at the appropriate moment fit her into place. In the other corner his first triangle had collapsed for lack of inner support (isn't this another dimension?) into maudlin accusation and justification, carefully avoiding the central point. Towelgirl had just been wooed, won and discarded by Estman and he was now—Ecks thought—trying to pass her on to me. Estman thinks he has wooed and won me, Towelgirl probably thought, so just to show him I'll shoot through with this Ecks. They're a bunch of no-hopers Eastman possibly thought—bugger them.

It worked out exactly as each of them didn't intend. Estman read Towelgirl's face, told her she was over-cautious, provincial and thought she was sitting on a goldmine. The very unoriginality of it was numbing. Ecks, he said, was scared to get involved, thought simple beer-swilling Aussies beneath him. Another train, maybe the down paper train, hooted over towards Fassifern, but by this time Ecks and Towelgirl were under the house, Host and Holden were arguing to clumsy blows over the last bottle of Tooheys Flag Ale and Estman was meticulously putting Mrs. Host to bed. The pants were off again and the towel underneath this time, but before they were half-way through they realised that they were only projections thrown up by Estman to suit a private formula, a shot-gun bedding.

"You were quick". It was neither a compliment nor a protest.

"Too quick". It was neither a question nor a statement.

"No". It was neither an affirmation nor a denial.

She was still breathing heavily.

"Your pant is very short".

"That's the latest fashion, you dill".

"All the easier to . . .".

They were back in the lounge-room, sharing the tin of

•

sardines. "You're the last one I expected". And about a week later: "I must be shikkered but yes I'll marry you". Did she really use slang or was it just the phonemes?

Ecks realised then what had happened. It was those domestic objects, their precise outlines never determined, which keyed the evening. They had spoken of family, of the overspill of domestic bric-à-brac that a man living on his own never accumulates, of a casualness about nails and dead men and old newspapers which a bachelor can only affect. To meet these objects at night is worse, particularly under those circumstances, primed by Estman whose only object, albeit a muzzy one, was to establish the infinity at which the parallel lines of himself and Mrs. Host were to meet (to hell with triangles). He had tried to hand it to her as casually as possible, spreading the towel, and her on it, with drunken precision, but when the non-moment came he waited for the objects, the old motor tyre, the empty tea-chests, the perfunctory gardening tools, to possess him, make him one of them, and it must have been some time then that he had initiated the complexity of mutual deception that had led to the unasked question that was now (then) sealed and assigned between them.

"Mind if I eat the last sardine? Put it out of its misery?"

"Help yourself".

Break it down, Joe, her eyes had said. Here I am and here I stay. And after what just happened, I mean you never know. . . .

"Indeed and you do not". Z 3 had come back into the lounge-room, and went over to pull the venetians against the hot morning sun. "You would have made a charming couple, if you'll forgive me saying so. Where was it herself was from now—Spain was it, or MEXICO? But then I suppose these au pair girls don't really want to settle down—it's not what they're here for now, is it? You'll maybe have better luck where you're going, though mind you there's some of us that never fall into the trap—just born with long unsatisfied noses like retrievers, bring them back for everyone else but divil a thing in it for yourself". He helped himself to another sardine.

"It wasn't like that at all", said Ecks.

"Of course not", said Z 3, "and it never is, or was. The exile's view of past emotion is as wrong as the exile's view of Faraway Bay, on which the sun never goes down. An emotion looking for a tail-hook, like a genie without his lamp. That au pair girl of yours now—you'll put the things you think you want to remember about her into a little tin box and throw away the rest. One or two nice things dug out of a heap of blanks and one or two nasty things dug out of the same heap to spice it up a bit, turn it into a roaring bouncing affair altogether. But for every kiss there was a wet teatowel passed from hand to hand (the nail-varnish on her right forefinger was always chipped), for every crisp volley of talk a scuffle for a lot of balls in the undergrowth . . . but here I am talking out of character again, what will become of me at all? It reminds me of the time I was doing duty for you as Loeghaire le Victorieux—though why you had to put decent Inish names into French always foxed me—and I was as insane as a college lecturer before we were finished. Weeks you kept me standing about on a public platform whilst you pretended to yourself and everyone else that you were interested in wisdom instead of women, that the book was really being written because you wanted to write it and not because you were using it as a spider's web to trap yourself and any other poor fly in an unbuttoned mood that happened to buzz along. That Mr. H. Jacet now—as decent a man as ever had a nicer house and nicer wife —you never gave him a chance. And Allen—well I never cared for that character but at least he had a bit of go in him. And the women? Well, you kept them all within arm's length and never gave them a chance to be anything other than the selves you created for them. If you ask me . . .".

"Well I did marry you", said Ecks.

"Yes you married me", she said, walking over to the window and opening the blind so that the hot morning sun slatted her like a toastrack.

The pale, i.e. sunny bands across her head, chest, waist and sardine tin were now unremittingly bands of Z 3. He waited with some interest to see which way the voice would come out but Z She remained silent. The last of the oil from the sardine tin dripped unctuously down on to the patch on the floor where the old stationmaster's old stool had worn a shallow hollow that could be seen quite clearly now that his tintawn had been rolled up and taken away. He tried to read, opening his paperback timetable at 8.06 / 8.36 / 9.06 / 9.41 but couldn't concentrate on the story—anyway he had guessed already that the 0-6-0T had done it. He picked up the paper, tomorrow's *Times* they call all these local rags the *Times,* and tried to hand it to himself as casually as possible, though it was a thing he hadn't studied in school, handing things casually when they are never handed any other way but casually and you couldn't offhand or casually think of the way to hand them uncasually. Perhaps this time he could get beyond

writings of

He opened the page, folded it neatly back along the crease and propping it carefully against the reassuring bulk of Sir John Daniel began:

•

10.

ANYONE possessing information on
the life and customs of the Druids cannot have failed to
have found in them much that suggests immediate rele-
vance to our own urban existence, and the percipient stu-
dent will in the course of his day-to-day experience
collect many examples of apparently secular practices
which suggest an unchallengable link with what Sir John
Daniel[1] has aptly named as "the recuperative buoyancy
of spirit, the imaginative genius and undying love of po-
etic utterance which are characteristics of the Cymric
race". A recent example may be quoted. An Inish Sunday
newspaper[2] recently published an article under the head-
ing NEW SALAD IS NAMED MRS. LEMASS. Those familiar with

---

[1] *The Philosophy of Ancient Britain,* London 1927, passim.
[2] Dick West: *The Sunday Review,* September 22, 1963, p. 16.

Celtic tradition will not need to be reminded of the correspondence of natural phenomena with the birth and deeds of mythological heroes. Two foals were dropped at the birth of Cuchullain, and the parallel of the salad endowed with the attributes of matriarchal leadership does not need to be emphasised. "Only rarely does one (recipe) muster sufficient acclaim to warrant enshrinement in a recipe book", says the newspaper report in its description of the new salad-symbol. One may perhaps be permitted at this juncture a legitimate speculation as to the number of lost symbols and natural correspondences which have failed to come down to us. The main animals have endured: the salmon, the wolfhound, the swan, simply perhaps because they were, so to speak, always in the eye of the beholder. To the dweller on the plains of Emain Macha the indeterminate symbolism of the salad must have been harder to grasp, less readily apprehended, whereas the salmon, the wolf-dog, the swan with its consubstantiality in every element except perhaps fire (though the Beltaine fires may indeed have served to roast one of the creatures for a king's delectation) were part of the day-to-day business of living. Françoise Le Roux speaks of "La magie végétale et la médecine magique" [3] with particular reference, of course, to the mistletoe, which was gathered in a great ceremony on the sixth day of the moon. It is not difficult to see the salad-gathering as a minor, perhaps almost a secular ceremony in which the victims of the accompanying sacrifice may perhaps have been lesser animals, the objectives equally unassuming. The Greek plural *salates* is quite possibly cognate with the

---

[3] *Les Druides*, Paris 1961, passim.

Latin *sancta vates* by elision and eclipsis of the affricative to the labial, and this is reflected in the Celtic equivalents,[4] hinting at the sacred nature of the plant in symbolical usage. On the other hand it would be premature at this point in our investigations to attempt to prove a direct parallel without the corroboration of further examples. A significant increase in the naming of salads for folk-heroes or heroines[5] might serve to indicate the re-emergence of a long-obscured tradition, but for unequivocal verification some evidence of continuing, if subsumed, observance would be required such as the practice of placing salad at the four corners of the marriage-bed or its playing a part in simple divination rites such as those practised with tea-leaves in current Inish superstition.[6] Pliny has pointed out[7] that the practice of vegetable veneration among the Gauls was widespread, and the con-

---

[4] Compare Irish *sailéad,* Welsh *bwydlys* and *bwyd,* victuals, which hints at a ceremonial connotation, as in the phrase *Mydrwyr yn canu ar en bwyd en hunain*—a cant phrase for a musical amateur (W. Owen Pughe: *A Dictionary of the Welsh Language,* Denbigh 1832). The *llys* root indicates something that separates, that parts off, that serves to discriminate—(cp. *llysaidd:* of a nature not to be touched), and also herbs and plants in the form *llysiau.* This is illustrated in the compounds *llysiau y llwynog*—stinking cranebill; *llysiau y cribau*—fuller's teasel; *llysiau y din*—biting arsemart; and perhaps most interesting of all, *llysiau yr oen*—lamb's lettuce. This may indicate an early fusion of Druidic and Christian traditions in relation to the salad ceremonies.

[5] But compare the absence of parallel development in dessert nomenclature following the initiation of the *Peach Melba.*

[6] Inish *cnámhoga.* The etymological significance of tea-cup reading as a vestige of more consciously magical rites may be seen by comparing the In. *cnaím:* to corrode, and *cnámh:* bone, with Scots Gaelic *cnàmh:* to corrode and *cnàimh:* bone; cf. the familiar Australian Aboriginal practice of *pointing the bone.* The confusion is suggestive.

[7] *Natural History,* XXV, 106.

temporary Cymric adherence to the leek may suggest a modern parallel. The Christian implantation of the shamrock as a national Inish symbol may simply have supplanted an earlier cult of the salad, and again this may be borne out by the continuing custom, in remote areas of western and southern Inish, of preparing a shamrock salad on the fifth Tuesday after March 29th in a leap year. The significance of the numbers (the five plus four for the leap year differentiated by the one of Tuesday—probably the first day of the Celtic nine-day week) reinforces the significance of the ancient observance which may be read as the dim survival of one of the last of the pagan challenges to the new religion.

"The basic ingredients of Salad Lemass are multi-shades of greens, beets, cucumbers and chopped eggs", the account continues, and quotes an unidentified comment, "It tastes good but it looks awful", in which the latter adjective is apparently used in its colloquial connotation of "bad" rather than in the etymological meaning "awe-inspiring".[8] This immediately recalls the passage in the Battle of Mag Tuired[9] which tells of the three hundred and sixty-five medicinal plants which sprang forth from Miach's grave after his killing by the druid Diancecht. The variegated nature of the "Mrs. Lemass" together with its putative therapeutic qualities ("It tastes good but it looks awful") is a simple reversal of a common reaction to medicinal preparations, and suggests an attempt to hark back to the symbolic as distinct from the nutritive application of food. There are parallels in contemporary

---

[8] Aw'ful: caufing an Awe, terrible apt to ftrike a Terror into—*An Universal Etymological Englifh Dictionary*; N. Bailey, London 1731.
[9] *Les Druides*, p. 64.

Inish in the consumption of Scots fermented liquors as a proof of greater wealth and social standing, though this latter instance may represent a subconscious urge to rediscover the elixir of forgetfulness as described in the *Serglige Cúchulainn* where it is said of Cuchulainn that "when he had drunk (of the elixir) he no longer remembered Fand nor anything he had done".[1] The hazel, the oak, the sorb or service-tree all played their part in Druidical ceremonies. Is it not likely that the arboriform salad, particularly the "everlasting" variety,[2] might have been employed in the humbler roles already adverted to, perhaps even in the course of early instruction of selected candidates for priestly office? It is worth noting finally that "Mrs. Lemass" was created (the choice of verb is interesting) in the United States of America *where scores of new salads are created every day* (mytalics). The selection principle is ruthless, but perhaps not to the extent of that which obtained in the Druidical era when, as far as can be at present ascertained, any clear reference to the salad in its symbolic or magical context failed to find its way into recorded literature or even, with one or two questionable exceptions, into the subsumed traditions of the Celtic race.

•————————————————

There was perhaps a parallel in the symbol for A in the bardic alphabet (s A L A d)—a fir tree, or inverted salad, and he was just turning to Sir John Daniel to verify the reference when he noticed that Z 3 was crouched over

---

[1] *Ogham* X, p. 310.
[2] Lettuce "Salad Bowl"—loose-leaved type for pulling, medium green. Strand's Superfine Seeds, 44 Strand, London.

the fireplace rekindling the fire with nine sticks. His cloak of bird-feathers rustled as he moved and he turned towards Mr. Ecks in a fall of mist so that everything except the two of them, the glowing fire and the reflective sardine tin disappeared. The wind rose outside, or rather around them because there was no longer an inside nor an outside, and through it the whistle of the o-6-oT could be apprehended, the doppler-ganger, the bird that lives in every element but one and carries that one within itself. Ecks looked at Z 3, whose eyes were now burning with the secret knowledge of a man who is sure of at least one identity.

"Question me", he said, "for I am a lover of women".

"It was a peculiarity of Math, son of Mathonwy, Lord of Gwynnedd, that he could live only if his feet were held in a maiden's lap", Z 3 replied. "We have no reverence for this condition in Arrack Mines".

"This is the omphalos, the still centre", Mr. Ecks replied divagationally, "which, as I have already ascertained, is orientated astronomically in the most propitious manner. In the manner of my coming, in the obscure nature of my birth—though the legend exists and is current in the Keflavik region of Southern Iceland that omens of great portent were observed by partial observers on that particular March 29th, that being a leap year—I am entitled to the privileges and restrictions of the hero: the defiance of the elements, the power of divination, and in particular the jus primae noctis with Miss Nicer O'Pair Girl, Hood Mrs. and child, Humphrey Mrs. and child and any and every five inches of nylon, which, coming down the gangplank into the wind becomes seven and a half inches and . . .".

"We have listened long and we have listened with impatience to your inhibited recollections of loves and half-loves", Z 3 interrupted, holding the sardine tin so that the reflected light from the nine-stick fire flickered unsteadily in Ecks's eyes. "In this country such revelations are neither proper nor acceptable. Your claim to be a lover of women cannot be admitted on logical grounds. Love to us implies a singular object. A plural object is an *argumentum ex homine*".

The mist began to thin. Ecks observed that he and Z 3 were travelling on an open platform truck on a narrow-gauge railway across a dark brown Inish bog. In the distance was the inward-looking omphalos shape of a concrete cooling-tower. Z 3's bird-feathers rustled in the wind.

"In a moment", he shouted through the thumping of the diesel engine, "we will be switched onto a branch line which will lead us directly to your first confrontation. This is your first task, and should you emerge from it successfully there will remain only two to complete the triad and release your spirit into eternity. You must call upon me neither for assistance nor advice. Have a sardine".

Ecks took one and sucked it thoughtfully. He had been vouchsafed a prevision of this trial, which would be nothing less than a direct confrontation with the triad of female deities which he himself had consecrated in Pitt Street, Sydney, Keflavik airport and a nicer house in one of the nicer roads in Arracker Mines. They would challenge him to complete his advertisement (for tomorrow's *Times* as they call all these local rags) in public view. He bit hard on a nubile backbone.

The train clattered over a junction, rounded a turf-stack and slowly drew to a halt on a siding which already

held a row of full trucks and offered good cover. Choosing his moment carefully Ecks leapt from the flat car exactly opposite a gap between two empty trucks on a parallel line and dived for cover as a hail of exacerbations re-
verberated on the rusting metal and embedded themselves deep in the stacked turf.

Cautiously he peered round the corner of the truck.
Ahead, about a hundred metres away, was the dim outline of a shunter's hut, fish-grey against the muddly sky-
line. Holding his 3/3 Bic at the ready he began to inch
forward, diving into the shelter of another truck as a well-
aimed vituperation grazed his subconscious. The siding
ended in makeshift buffers about thirty metres from the
hut, leaving a stretch of open ground which must be covered at a dash if he were to stand any chance at all. The
last truck on the line was luckily almost empty, and climb-
ing onto the coupling at the unexposed end he managed
to roll over the top into it to the accompaniment of a fresh
colley of well-directed abuse. These girls were certainly
very handy with their weapons.

He crouched on the cold metal floor of the truck and by
inching slowly forward until his eye was on a level with a
grommet-aperture (clearly labelled FAINNE TEADÁIN in
Inish) was able to see into the one window of the hut,
which was now slightly below him though still thirty
metres away.

Nothing moved. The hut was apparently deserted. Carefully lowering himself again, cursing his carelessness for
not having come to Inish better prepared, Ecks slowly
raised his 3/3 Bic and rested it on the lip of the fainne
teadáin. Taking careful aim, he fired.

ANYONE!—the first shot spattered hollowly against

the sill of the hut. There was no response. Ecks shifted his position slightly on the cold floor of the truck and fired again.

POSSESESSING!—the shot this time went cleanly through the window with a faint tinkle of glass. There was a muted scream from within, quickly hushed.

Ecks waited in silence. Somewhere behind him a seagull wheeled, screamed, then dived low over him so that he could hear the feathers combing the wind. In front of him a scoop of heavy mist began to roll off the mountain. In an hour, perhaps two hours, perhaps five hours, it would be dark. He must act.

Cautiously and with meticulous precision he began to lower his 3/3 Bic from the lip of the fainne teadáin. He checked the magazine. Good. Seven shots left—an appropriate number. He edged slowly towards the rear of the truck, the end furthest away from the hut, but froze suddenly as his left foot refused to move any further behind him. Had he been hit? He experienced a tense moment of anxiety, an anxious moment of tension, a momentary tensile angst, until he discovered that his shoelace had caught on a protruding bolt on the floor of the truck. He breathed again—and again—and moved delicately until he was crouching close against the back of the vehicle, timing his spring. Everything was quiet. In far-off Pitt Street Hood Mrs. wheeled, screamed and dived low under the pram containing and Child as the tram rattled towards her. In far-off Keflavik airport Pierre Bernard checked his magazine in the airport bookshop. In front of him a scoop that he had missed was being rolled off to the ancien rédacteur en chef. With a sigh Ecks timed his spring for the last time, got up and stepped quickly and quietly over the back of the truck, ducking down behind it as soon as his feet touched the squelchy bog. He peered carefully round it towards the hut, but nothing stirred. Thin smoke from the cooling-tower began to drift towards him. The wind —from the sea—was freshening. In an hour, or two hours, or five hours, it would lay an effective smoke screen across the thirty metres of unprotected ground. He waited.

His opportunity came just eight seconds later. A sudden belch from the cooling-tower dropped a saffron curtain between him and the hut and the mountain. He darted forwards into it, his feet making no noise on the squelchy bog, but when he was about halfway across the intervening space there was a blinding flash. He pitched forward and, for just eight seconds, knew no more.

When he came to, Z 3 was bending over him.

"Could you not look where you're going?", he complained. "You nearly stretched me that time. Here, grab a hold of this and get moving"—and he handed Ecks his 3/3 Bic which had fallen into the squelchy bog and gave him a push in the general direction of the hut, offering him a sardine which Ecks ignored as he rapidly covered the remaining distance that separated him from his goal.

He flattened himself with a dull thud against the wooden wall, and swinging his right arm round to the open window emptied the last seven shots into the darkened interior without taking aim.

INFORMATION ON THE LIFE AND WRITINGS OF—they reechoed off the mountain, now almost completely hidden by mist, and died away into the patterned Inish silence. Nothing moved.

Ecks waited. It seemed like eight seconds but was in fact one, two or five hours before he edged painstakingly

to his right, caught the latch of the door in his free hand—
though his 3/3 Bic was useless now and in any case would
be no match for a 6H Faber-Castell—and flung it open.
He went in.

The three of them were lying motionless on the floor.
He rushed forward and pressed his chest to their ears,
each in turn. Thank God, he was still breathing. For the
next hour, or two hours, or eight seconds he worked fever-
ishly until by the time he had finished the footnote to a
footnote in chapter five. (*The number 29 as significant
of a state of temptation, trial or probation, cf. Daniel, op.
cit., pp. 113-4*) all three showed signs of reviving. He
made them as comfortable as possible, one in each corner
of the hut, bearing in mind letters in the newspapers on
the question of modesty in dress, mostly concerned with
women's apparel and modern fashions. Many and varied
protests are seen from time to time from women (or girls)
who maintain there is nothing wrong with the scanty
skirts, very short shorts, plunging necklines and other
"fashions" being adopted by some—repeat some—of our
young women. Then he sat down in the other corner
and looked at them.

The first thing he noticed, as he was meant to, was that
their features were identical—but he had expected as
much and this came as no surprise. It would be a relief
not to have to watch himself parade a different character
for each one in turn: the misunderstood boy, the enig-
matic scholar, Neil Issagum the Inish-Amnesian mystery
man. The next thing he noticed was that their bodies, although attractively positioned (he had been unable to
resist one or two artistic touches) stirred no feeling in him
whatsoever—they might have been three aunt's compan-

ions putting out dustbins on a wet day in one of the nicer streets of Arracker Mines. This withdrawal of a simple, reliable and issue-evading stimulus was unexpected, and it left him with the prospect of having to talk to them, if they came to, as people rather than as women. He hoped they wouldn't, but knew that the geasa was inescapable.

"It's a great geasa", said Z 3 from the doorway, his beady eyes bright on each side of his beak. "You can't ask one the crucial question without asking all three, yet the three as one can ask *you* three different questions. It's an arrangement that has proved popular in many theological systems. Have a little salad with your sardine?"

Ecks waved him away and went on waiting. Closing his eyes he tried for an easy take-off into suspended animation, hands on pullover inside raincoat through double pockets, ankles crossed as if chained, neck sunk into collar like broken lead soldier mended with a matchstick. His last glimpse of the world was the grey distant coast, just like any other in the rain. He missed the five inches of nylon, which

"Not that way, please—that is too easy"—the figure in the corner directly opposite had spoken with the voice of Miss Girl.

"I'm trying to introduce you as casually as possible", replied Ecks. "I'm trying to get you to say to one another what you would never say to me, trying to unwrap each of you to vanishing-point to see which disappears first, risking the knowledge of how much of me will go off with each of you. I'm trying to overhear you in a conversation that can only happen next March 29th when you have read the advertisement in tomorrow's"

"You came about an advertisement, isn't it?"—the voice

from the left-hand corner was that of Hermosilla Jacet.

"Too bloody right he did"—from the right-hand corner.
"And you can put that away"—as Ecks made a move for
his 3/3 Bic—"it's man to shiela now".

ANYONE . POSSESSING . INFORMATION . ON . THE . LIFE .
AND . WRITINGS . OF—Ecks counted the spent shells on
the floor. Then he turned and faced all three of them.

"You all know what must come next as well as I do", he
said, overdoing the Amnesian accent. "I must give myself
a name, state my credentials, establish my co-ordinates,
offer each one of you a separate accommodation address
to which you may direct your replies. But you are all the
same person—I have known that for a long time. And the
fact that you who are three have proved to be one means
that I who have thought I was one must in fact be three—
and the advertisement can make no provision for alterna-
tives. You have obsessed me separately, individually in
different ways—ways which I cannot relate now for fear
of making one or more of you blush even though you are
all the same person. But you have each withdrawn in different directions leaving me with no more than the
shadow of an obsession which I have tried to expiate in
auto-erotic activities such as those which I for a time practised in Pitt Street with the not-telephone BL 4586 beside me when I did not understand English very well
and . . .".

"Stick to the point", said Z 3, wheeling and screaming
outside the window.

"Of course", replied Ecks. The three women had heard
him in silence and continued to hear his silence in silence.
Ecks took a deep breath:

"This has to be said, although you know it and I know

it already. You are the three whom I never intended to reply to the advertisement that I never intended to finish. Others I was prepared to hear from: relicts of an Amnesian childhood; a New Australian's cobbers; a pornographer's mates; a fellow-raiser of the veil which has covered. But not from people who may unseal the carefully-papered cracks, unstick a forgotten envelope or perform some other straightforward act of betrayal that would have all the reality of metaphor. I am a successful Amnesian businessman, reported in the leading Inish newspapers to have bought Arrack Mines station which was closed to all traffic ecks years ago next March 29th, next March being a leap year. But I cannot put that in the advertisement, the next word of which must be a proper noun. And the question remains—what is proper? You, Miss Girl (he had forgotten from which figure Miss Girl's voice had emanated so bowed discriminately to all three) know me as the tenant of attractive semi-detached family residence of character on bus route, convenient to shops, schools, churches. Accommodation comprises. But through my dusky window I no longer acknowledge that nicer self, nor my nicer wife, nicer children, and certainly not my nicer au pair girl. You were to be the last, the final echo of Pitt Street, Sydney, Keflavik airport and of course MAYA DE MEXICO. . . .

"Stick to the point", screamed Z 3, wheedling outside the window.

"Of course", replied Ecks. "And then regarding the matter of my wife (he nodded at a point plotted by dropping a perpendicular into each of the three women) I shall of course make no statement. Everything in marriage is said in the first fortnight. The rest of the relationship is a

•

futile attempt to unsay it. And that leaves . . .".

But he could no longer be certain about the identity of the third lady. Names flitted through his mind, shapes of ears, lips, laughter, whiffs of perfume, toothpaste, damp nylon, hot sheets, words and looks that cut and stabbed. *She* would never have replied anyway. He tried: tried to hand her the paper, which he still had in his pocket, as casually as possible, it's a thing you don't study in school, handing things casually when they are never handed any other way but casually and you couldn't offhand or casually think of the way to hand them uncasually, but the dialogue presented a problem and she just looked blankly at tomorrow's *Times*, they call all these local rags the *Times*:

"I'm sorry but I don't remember anyone of that name. I possess no information".

"The question has been answered before it has been asked", said Z 3 at the window, "in conformity with the best Druidical principles". He picked fragments of sardine off his feathers with his long, probing beak. "The first part of the ordeal has been completed. You have the choice of either vanishing yourself, returning by rail, or closing your eyes and letting everything around you subside into the mist which, you will notice, is once more rolling off the mountain. I recommend the latter as being the least tiring in view of your future commitments".

"Question me", said Ecks, "for I am a lover of my country".

"That comes later", replied Z 3. "No man has a right to march to the boundary of a nation without giving due notice. We will go into all that". Ecks shut his eyes.

There was a hiss of steam, reminiscent of the 150 lb.

boiler pressure of 4-4-0 no. 57, total heating surface 1,027 sq. ft., grate area 19.68 sq. ft., and they began to move. Ecks settled back and watched the scenery flicker past outside his eyelids.

"Question me", he repeated, "for I am a lover of my country".

"The penalty for making use of your faculties when the geasa is in motion is four leap years in Keflavik airport. But we'll be home in no time at all, since it appears that this train does not stop at Knoppoge, Knoppoge North, Derryra Beg, Derryra More, Ayle, Derrico, Ardcullen, Ardcullenmarshes, Ahanure North, Ahanure South, Courtnabooly West, Monadubbaun, Drinagh Intake, Gibberwell, Graiguesallagh, Shanoo, Horesland, Ballyfinoge Great, Jacketstown, Loughsollish, Minnauns, Dirtystep, Bawnkeal, Lissataggle, Knockaneacoolteen, Glannafunshoge, Mountjuliet, Knockbutton, Kylefreaghane or Arabela. Have a sardine salad—I'm afraid there's no buffet car on the train".

"Mine's an arrack", said Ecks hopefully; but the bottle for some reason seemed to be empty. There was nothing to do but wait.

11.

SOLD by private treaty—Z 3 ripped the auctioneer's notice off the window as he put down the traps.

"Well, here we are, lads. On behalf of Mr. Ecks, successful Amnesian businessman, I welcome you one and all to Arrack Mines. Look lively there now—this station has a tradition of punctuality to maintain".

They followed him over the threshold—Z 3 with the old grip that had caused so much trouble in Keflavik airport; Mr. J. Hackett with the battered suitcase that had caused so much trouble in Pitt Street, Sydney, when it flew open on a North Shore tram to bring to light long-buried treasures of wisdom, viz.: a pile of novels of inferior quality; and Allen O'Girl with nothing but a paper under his right arm—the *Times* as I think they call this local rag. I brought up the rear, as befitted an Amnesian beneficiary under the Undeveloped Stations Act.

My first impressions were not enthusiastic. At the auction it was full of people, the auctioneer like a judge raised above us on the old stationmaster's old high desk, faces of small boys peering through the window from the platform; but now in the failing Inish March 29th light I could see the worn patch where feet had waited to buy tickets, the worn patch where feet had waited to sell tickets, the tickets which had perhaps been trodden into a gap in the boards by the last fare-paying feet. Z 3 and Hackett and O'Girl were standing around a little uncomfortably having laid down the traps, though O'Girl was still holding the paper—which he had whisked with a grin neatly under his right arm with another of those unplanned movements of which one of my ancestral furriers would strongly have disapproved. I tried to imagine the correct Inish gesture that the occasion demanded. Perhaps my recent Pitt Street experiences would stand me in good stead.

"Who's for a jar, lads?", I enquired in my careful Inish idiom, "or would you prefer a little light pornography?" The perfect Amnesian host.

"It's thirsty weather all right", replied O'Girl, whom I shall call Allen. He had carried his paper, as casually as possible, all the way from Z 3's car to the station entrance.

Hackett looked round expectantly, as if expectantly expecting the expected drink to materialise from the oil-stained press in the corner, which was where the storm-lanterns might have been kept and which was where the drink probably would be when I had managed to balance my battered suitcase on some kind of souvenir-fulcrum

•

and open it. Oh, yes, I had it—not so green as I'm cabbage looking: another useful idiom.

"Oh, yes, I have it", I said, "not as green as I'm lettuce looking. Now if I can just find somewhere to balance the suitcase and open it . . .".

"Lend a hand there now, lads", Z 3 shuffled forward, "it's in a good cause".

Together we pulled the old stationmaster's old desk out from the wall where it had been pushed and propped the suitcase on top of it. I clicked the catches.

"I see you're a reading man", observed Hackett, as the open lid revealed a pile of novels of inferior quality.

"Ah yes, I'm a great one for the pornography", I retorted. "Have you read this one: MEN BECOME INSANE, by College Lecturer? There's some hot stuff in that". I began to flick over the pages.

"There'll be time enough for that kind of thing", put in Z 3 (I thought a little nervously). "Where's the jar?"

I dug down beneath some hastily-packed souvenirs—a tin of curmudgeon in its own juice from Keflavik, a packet of everlasting clitoris, until my fingers touched glass. "Here we are", I announced proudly, "best Australian arrack, made in Pitt Street, Sydney, by Amnesian exiles. I think you will find it rather interesting, my friends".

My friends looked puzzled but respectful.

"Glasses", said Z 3, "we need glasses".

Hackett was peering shortsightedly at the label, holding his umbrella by the stem like a lorgnette.

"I never heard tell of that before", he observed; "but sure you can only die once".

I dug into the suitcase again, found a toothmug and

surreptitiously shaking out the teeth pulled it out and stood it on the desk.

"There's one for a start: any further contributions, gentlemen?"

"Hold hard", said Z 3, "I think I have something in the old car". And he was off.

We waited in a restrained silence. Hackett and Allen, friends of Z 3, I scarcely knew as yet. I had been introduced to them in Shenanagan's, where I had found myself after the auction in Z 3's company. We each debated whether we should say something.

"Well", said Allen, who finished his debate a little ahead of the rest of us, "I'd say you should do well here, a business like yours I mean: low outgoings, no overheads, and a fat government grant to keep you in wealth and idleness for the rest of your natural. It would almost make a man be inclined to change his nationality".

I pondered the point while Hackett was finishing his debate and preparing to speak. I had a spurious and obsessive concept of nationality, like all uprooted Amnesians. Would this be my country? Would the first sip of arrack turn to Inish mist on my lips?

Hackett finished his debate a little ahead of me. "In no time at all you'll be looking round for a nicer house and nicer wife to go with it. You're not a married man, I believe?"

But at that moment Z 3 returned bearing two dusty and handle-less tea cups. "Just what the doctor ordered", he announced. "Best Royal Tara—fit for a king".

There was a moment of embarrassment as we all realised that the tally was still only three. "Host drinks from the bottle!", I announced, "an old Amnesian custom!"

Gravely I measured out three equal quantities, as near as I could judge, into the waiting receptacles. Z 3 grasped his—the toothmug—bravely. "A toast", he proclaimed, "to the old D. & S.E.R.—long may it continue to run on Amnesian lines".

I thanked them for their very few kind words and watched them while they drank; and then, because their instinctive Inish attitudes made me feel once more alien, I raised the bottle to my lips, closing my eyes so that I would not see their grimaces at the unfamiliar and probably unpleasing taste, giving them time to reassume the necessary expressions of politeness.

"That's hard stuff"—Z 3 was first off the mark, as usual.

"Very interesting". Hackett was studying his half-empty glass.

"It's wet—and it's warm". Allen the businessman. "How about getting the fire going? There's a load of old rubbish would be better out of the way". And he began kicking a pile of dusty papers over towards the grate in the corner.

"No, don't burn those", I interposed rather too quickly. "There may be something of historical interest".

Allen looked up quickly. "Old timetables, old newspapers, and the old stationmaster's old boots. Ancient history, my friend, must make way for the new régime: Ecks Import-Export. What the hell are you going to import-export anyway?"

"This and that", I replied. "Souvenirs of Inish, made in Keflavik. Holy pictures of Pierre Bernard, ancien rédacteur en chef. The latest batch of MAYA DE MEXICO bear greatest individuality of design. And Inish mist to satisfy the requirements of the grant. In no time at all I shall be looking out for a nicer house, nicer wife, nicer children and perhaps nicer au pair girl. Let me know if you hear of anything. I might even put an advertisement in the paper".

It was with difficulty that I persuaded them to refill their glasses, but after that the bottle emptied itself, like the top half of an egg-timer, unassisted. Allen, disregarding my protests, had made a fire with the débris in the narrow grate, though I had managed to souvenir perhaps two or three timetables and some segments of an official notice which had been ripped off the wall. It would come in useful. The boots saved themselves. As the dark Inish March 29th evening ebbed into night the bare room began to take on something of the intimacy of permanence. The few objects that I had unpacked, or had unpacked themselves, sat firmly in their positions with the assertion of usage. The old stationmaster's old rolltop desk began to shape itself to my horizon, so that I could look out over it to Pitt Street, to Keflavik airport, to Pierre Bernard ancien rédacteur en chef—and they had assumed the reassurance of false perspective so that I could keep them firmly in their planes: yesterday, the day before, four years ago next March 29th, next March being a leap year. Our four cylinders were now firing a good deal more smoothly than those of Z 3's ancient car, and anecdote followed anecdote: business from Allen, domestic from Hackett, Inishphilosophical from Z 3—and Amnesian-Australian from Ecks—advancing of their own momentum. But quite suddenly the movement ceased.

"A dead man?", commented Z 3, holding up the arrack bottle. "But the night is young. Suppose I were to shoot off in the old car down to Shenanagan's and bring back a dozen. How about it, lads?"

•

We assented with one voice, and whilst Z 3 departed on his mission of mercy Hackett, Allen and myself strolled out of the old stationmaster's old office and on to the platform in search of a breath of air. It was a still Inish March 29th night. The 5.45 p.m. from the city had not just stopped and disgorged its usual complement of old businessmen who had grown decrepit with their trains. We watched them in sentimental silence, each busy with his own thoughts.

My own thoughts (I cannot vouch for those of my companions) were connected with the new country whose delights I was about to experience. As I looked at the fading blue of the mountains and listened to the purling of the golden latreens I was reminded, because it was so different, of my first glimpse of Keflavik airport, cold and shrunken behind its bastions of lava, and of Pitt Street, Sydney, lone and sinuous between Circular Quay and Central Railway. How I had envied that stalwart citizen of Hafnarfjordur, secure in his thousand-year nationality, phonetically impregnable in the purity of his language, tamped in with tradition; and how I had envied that Wooloomooloo bodgie waiting for the tram, so secure in his nationality that he could spit at New Australians, triphthong-true to his language, never fearing to speak of the days of '88. And now here was I, attempting to lift the veil that has covered Druidism for centuries . . . but the return of Z 3 cut short my unprofitable musings.

"Let's have them out here", he suggested, depositing two sugar bags on the platform and proceeding to remove the contents. "Hold your hats on, boys—there goes the express!"

In respectful silence we watched it pass, the double

frames and outside cranks of 2-4-0 no. 14 flashing in the still Inish March 29th air. It disappeared down the down line, its 5 ft. 6 in. diameter wheels and 14 in. by 22 in. cylinders beating out a nostalgic rhythm.

"That's the last for the night", remarked Hackett, who had said little during Z 3's absence, "now we can drink in peace".

But it wasn't. Suddenly the roadbed on the Up line began to vibrate and tingle, and then amid the clatter of connecting rods and a hiss of steam a magnificent 4-4-0 passenger engine built by Kitson & Co. in 1896-7, numbered 53 and named *Jubilee* in honour of the fiftieth anniversary of the Company, pulled in and drew to a halt.

"She's a stranger in these parts", remarked Allen. "Built for working the Loch Garman boat trains on the main line. Cylinders 17 in. by 24 in., coupled wheels 6 ft. in diameter, 8 ft. 3 in. wheelbase, bogy of the pendulum link type. Wonder what brings her here?"

We had little time, however, to think about the locomotive, total heating surface 994 sq. ft., for two figures had descended from the first coach and when the train had pulled away from the platform and rumbled off up the line they were revealed as Mr. Ecks and his friend Z 3, obviously returning from a trip to the country.

"Well now, and what brings you two boyos here at this time of night?", asked Mr. J. Hackett when they had crossed the line without bothering to use the footbridge and were standing before us.

"A special", said Z 3 brusquely—"she came straight through". I thought he sounded a trifle piqued, and his feathers were distinctly ruffled.

I was more worried, however, by Ecks's appearance. It

•

would be four years next March 29th, next March being a leap year, since I had last set eyes on him, and I thought he had aged. I knew, of course, that he had been spending a lot of time on his Druidical researches, even neglecting his import-export business to do so, and I began to fear that it was telling on his health. I presumed, too, that this latest excursion had something to do with his investigations.

"You must know the country better than a native by now", I said to him jokingly: "Inishiores Inishiis ipsis, as I believe the phrase goes".

He seemed not to have heard me.

"Question me", he said, turning to Z 3, "for I am a lover of my country".

If it was a joke I couldn't understand it, and neither, I must admit, could Allen or Mr. H. Jacet. Perhaps it was the translation of an Amnesian proverb—several people had remarked that Ecks's thoughts seemed to be turning more and more to the past of late and that his speech was frequently peppered with unrecognisable triphthongs. Z 3, however, replied rather snappishly: "We'll go into all that later"—or words to that effect. And he added: "Would one of you bowsies ever offer me a drink?"

One of us passed him a bottle—he was never a one to worry about the niceties—but Ecks wouldn't take anything, saying that these days he drank nothing but arrack, or something of the sort. You could see with half an eye that the man was going to pieces. His thick shock of strong chestnut hair that was combed in a jaunty quiff over his thick, strong, jaunty right eyebrow was greying a little over his aristocratically pallid temples. He was perhaps forty, perhaps not, a fine tall stocky figure of a man, but

his stoop was more noticeable now than his attractive Amnesian accent. I went over to him, profiting from a moment when the others were engaging in a discussion on
Druidism in its contemporary manifestations (I don't hold
with that class of talk myself) and took him by the arm.

"Would you like to step inside?", I asked him, "I've a
drop of the hard stuff".

"Well that's very kind of you Ecks yes", he replied,
"it's quite cool for March 29th and I found the journey
rather tiring".

It was gloomy inside the old stationmaster's old office,
but I explained that I could not light the gas-bracket (on
which, funnily enough, my tie was still hanging) as the
gas had been turned off in preparation for my departure.

"You're going?", he enquired—uneasily I thought, peering at me over the top of his imposing rolltop desk.

"Yes", I replied. "I shall have been here four years next
March 29th, next March being a leap year, and I feel
that's long enough. Not that I haven't done very nicely,
all things considered. Quite apart from my little import-
export business—and your Bord an tAma were very generous to me—I have made substantial progress with my
pornographic writings, in fact I was working on them up
to the last minute"—and he held up his well-fingered copy
of Sir John Daniel, ancien rédacteur en chef.

I poured him a stiff sardine oil, noticing that there was
very little left in the tin.

"Just before you go", I said, "I wonder whether you
would be good enough to help me out with something—
I'm afraid my Inish isn't quite up to it, even after four
years. It's just a little advertisement I'm putting in tomorrow's Times (I wonder why they call all these local rags

•   136

the *Times*?). You see I've got as far as ANYONE POSSESSING INFORMATION ON THE LIFE AND WRITINGS OF . . .".

But just then, of course, Z 3 had to totter into the old stationmaster's old office from the platform outside, I thought rather the worse for wear.

"Sneak away by yourself, would you?", he accused me, "and on your last evening with your old friends! Come on out now and enjoy the balmy March 29th air with the rest of us—you'll only be getting morbid sitting in here on your own".

But I could not enter his mood. Suddenly the thought of having arrived in yet another new country began to depress me. I could feel that another barrier had formed, that I would be more of a stranger here than I was in Pitt Street where I was more of a stranger than I was in Keflavik airport where I was more of a stranger than I will ever be to Mr. H. Jacet who will always label me an Amnesian, a foreigner, never a stranger who can then through his temerity in investigating such a dangerous and intolerable subject come to be regarded in a very uncomplimentary light and thus as a friend. I had noticed on the way here that I had not troubled to notice that the kerbstones were different from those employed in Pitt Street which were different from those which were not employed in Keflavik airport and I knew then that my journey had reached its furthest point and that the rest of the way would be back, back towards that Amnesian childhood of which I do not even now care to speak, back, back so that the present is always becoming further away as age pushes me backward towards my youth and the irritating habits I would have seen in my own son, Pilkington Master H., and which I would have watched him grow out of

—the deliberate diphthongisation of non-Inish triphthongs he had picked up from his father, for instance—I now see in myself: how I am more Amnesian when excited than I intend to be, how I manipulate portions of my body when talking on the telephone, and I know that though this will not deter me from attempting to lift the veil that has covered Druidism for centuries (for I am persuaded that, like the opening of the Egyptian tombs, something may be disclosed worthy of our admiration) it is less likely that it may bring to light long-buried advertisements.

"I know what it is", said Z 3, poking the fire of timetables into a reluctant blaze, "you're annoyed with me because I didn't give you a straight answer to your question —the one about loving your country or whatever it was. Now there's one thing we always tell our visitors, and I'll pass it on as a piece of good advice even if you are intending to settle down like—y'know? Never get into an argument either about politics or druidism. That way you'll stay out of trouble till you know your way around. Come on outside now and join the party. Sure it's too nice an evening to be frowsting over the ol' fire".

He was exaggerating the Inish exaggeration, and he meant it unkindly, but I still couldn't recapture the party spirit. Would I ever be on equal terms with these men who were so casually drinking on my platform? I could feel my Amnesian punctiliousness, which no amount of Pitt Street grogging on had been able to dissipate, beginning to re-assert itself—I wanted to take them apart as an arm, a gesture, a slurred vowel, rather than accept them instantly all of a piece.

Z 3 went out again, his feathers rather huffily ruffled, and I heard him exchanging banter with Hackett and

Allen out on the platform until their voices were drowned by the hiss and clank of what must have been a down special (freight? I counted the clinkety-clanks over the joints) and I turned once more to look at Ecks, who was standing staring moodily at the gas-bracket (the gas had been turned off in preparation for my departure) as if he were contemplating hanging himself from it with my own tie, which funnily enough was still hanging on it. He was the first to speak.

"I would have thought that after four years—next March 29th *is* a leap year, isn't it?—you would have progressed a little further in your study of that which was to the Jews a stumbling-block, and unto the Greeks foolishness. Your station, in terms of the omphalos, is ill-orientated. Your knowledge, like your sardine oil, is ill-digested. Your conduct has been ill-regulated. Several times recently I've read letters in the newspapers on the question of modesty in dress, mostly concerned with women's apparel and modern fashions. Your attempt to lift the veil that has covered Druidism for centuries has resulted in the discomfiture of my friend Z 3 and some very ineffectual pornography—as my friends Burrow and Klein will bear out. I think that the sooner you are gone the better".

I was delighted with this, though of course I took good care not to show it. For the first time for four years next March 29th Ecks had come out with it straight, and in a manner that left no room for cavilling about the cultivable potentialities of Miss Nicer O'Pair Girl, the Keflavik reminiscences of Mr. H. Jacet, ancien rédacteur en chef, the duplicity of Pilkington, Mrs. D., the phrasing of the advertisement I had been trying to write for tomorrow's *Times* and which I had (oh, yes, they call all these local

rags the) taken no further than ANYONE possessing information on the life and writings of

I must have spoken my thoughts aloud, for he froze in
his corner, to which he had moved from the gas-bracket,
and his voice was noticeably more rigid:

"I hope, Ecks", he said, "that you are not intending to
proceed with this infantile scheme? I tried to hand it to
you as casually as possible, that's a thing you don't study
in school, handling things as casually as possible, but I
wasn't sure that you could offhand or uncasually think of
the way to handle them uncasually. You have been trying
hard to connect, to put the pieces of Mr. H. Jacet and
Pierre Bernard ancien rédacteur en Pitt Street together in
their proper order, but you have lacked the basic sympathy to forgive the missing umbrella, the period 1936-1946
when he was unexplainedly absent in Keflavik airport;
to lift the veil that covered your nicer au pair girl and
make of her"

"An advertisement", I retorted hotly: "advertisements,
they were all advertisements—you'll see them all in tomorrow's *Times*. I was only asking them to believe in me,
to return the simple answer to the simple question ANYONE
possessing informat . . .".

"You have forgotten the third question", interrupted Z
3, reappearing through the door to the platform with a
stout bottle held like a wrong-ended telescope.

"Question me", Ecks repeated mechanically, lowering
his forehead until it touched the fingered but asceptic
cover of Sir John Daniel, "for I am a lover of myself".

"Grand evening", mouthed Mr. H. Jacet through the
dusky stationmaster's window.

•

12.

ECKS. February 29th 1936-1946 at the Arrack Mines Nursing Home to Hermosilla and Pierre Bernard Ecks, of Nicer House, Nicer Road, a son, Deo . . .

•

Gratias is a girl's name, surely? But it's too late now. He would have grown up an Inishman, comfortably orotund phonemes, sheltered from fragmentation by an address at Nicer House, Nicer Road, Arrack Mimes and the loving care of the erstwhile Miss Girl, whom of course he would never have seen taking off her clothes preparatory to taking a bath. For him Pitt Street, Sydney would have been a name on the map of Iceland, to be stabbed at with a pin in moments of tedium, not relived more and more painfully as the flesh withers from the memory and only the stark bones are left: the femur of a major embarrassment at a party with too-correct New Australian manners, the sacroiliac of mocking a revered national institution, (the directionless grooves of the tin roof), the tibia that prevented the honest proposal and provoked the anomalous one

"You were quick"—it was neither a compliment nor a protest.

"Too quick"—it was neither a question nor a statement.

"No". It was neither an affirmation nor a denial.

Pitt Street is almost gone—a whiff of pornography, the grind of a tram, a tatter of torn underwear (or was it the bathers the last time?), a face that will no longer own up to a name, a name that floats somewhere out over the low, flat rocks at Dee Why, which are themselves real now perhaps only for half a second a year when a hardness in the Inish summer air mingles with a cold taste of beer mingles with a new haircut mingles with a tangible excitement mingles with a staccato headline in tomorrow's *Times* mingles with the taste of spring roll through salt and kisses and the dip in the road at where was it oh yes Maidensbrush Creek . . . how many variables, what odds? The likelihood of co-ordination, of hitting the combination, grows more and more remote as the cogs move more slowly, mesh more reluctantly. The spring roll, for instance—they don't make them in Inish and it's four years next March 29th since I tasted one. And Maidensbrush Creek—somewhere on the road to Keflavik airport, out on that stony desert beyond Hafnarfjordur, the lava piled like fossilised dog droppings, the snows of Hekla disconcertingly white. And I have been in this island, in the import-export business, for four years next March being a leap year. I like that, it has pared down the anniversaries to a needle-sharp four-faceted point, but I never really learnt to live with Allen, with his complaints to the customs over the Mexican consignment, his shady discussions with fat, pork-fed men in drab mid-afternoon pubs with the radio muttering on the back shelf among the flyblown showcards, the curate endlessly polishing the same glass and outside the underpowered rain falling on small, tinny cars and wisps of bent straw from long-past bullocks. This island dies in mid-afternoon, buses hang impotently at termini, the paving stones are prepared with thin brown mud for the lithographic printing of lassitude, it is then that I long for the difference which of course I cannot now remember that was Dee Why, the cruel, stinging afternoon sun blown out of the continent at you by a westerly wind, the thirty-degree slump (was that Fahrenheit or Celsius?) that followed the Southerly Buster, the sudden brutal battering of rain transformed in seconds into rushing storm-water. Or the clear cold of Keflavik, coming at you unexpectedly round corners, the all-night insomnia of summer twilight, so like the determined insomnia of that party in Toronto with the siren of the train somewhere over towards Fassifern a D-55 Class with Cylinders 22″ × 26″, 51″ coupled wheels, grate area 28¾ sq. ft., Length Overall 60′ 11″. . . .

You were quick, it was neither a compliment nor a protest.
Too quick, it was neither a question nor a statement.
No. It was neither an affirmation nor a denial.

but I was remembering—was I remembering?—Allen and his failure to communicate with the pork-fed Inishmen stuffed tight into their shiny suits, insulated with their fat woolly pullovers. Allen was too ambitious, búsquelas en nuestras tiendas, and they all should have come running, but what Inishman, as he discovered to his cost, will discuss business over a brisk pot of breakfast coffee at the reasonable hour of 8.06 / 8.36 / 9.06? No, it must be in the dead afternoon, with the flabby brown rings congealing in the glasses, the top-heavy pints that move downwards, downwards O so slowly while Allen sipped his arrack and tried to make it last, trying to outsilence the other with words that meant nothing, the endless commentary on the climate, or weather as they call it, imagine referring to sunshine in the middle of Pitt Street in the middle of a business conversation they would rightly call you a dill if not a drongo but again I have forgotten the words. Or in Iceland either: the eruption of Hekla perhaps—Heklas Heklugos or something the man in the seat in front of me was reading. But this Allen could never, I fear, understand, having learnt his business methods in a harder school—Pierre Bernard, ancien rédacteur en chef—which put more emphasis on the grin and the underhand motion, another of those unplanned movements which some furry ancestor must have practised for days with a bone and a plantain leaf. He tried, after a while, to handle it as casually as possible, but could never quite reach that Inish level of casualness which is so distinct from the Pitt Street level of casualness which is almost entirely physical, the Inish level of casualness being something of a little onanist ritual, impossible for the newly-arrived Amnesian to penetrate. At least this is the conclusion that Allen came to, though naturally his sexual disappointments as well as his business setbacks cannot be said to have modi-

•   **144**

fied his unfavourable impression of the country. He always considered himself a practical man, with a record of successes in both fields in MAYA DE MEXICO, Keflavik and Pitt Street, Sydney, but he could be said to have added little to his collection of trophies during his residence in Inish. Does the climate of the country force young women to don shorts, some of which are so revealing as to be little better than a swimsuit? Hardly. Is a woman any the more charming or graceful for a backless dress, or a daringly low neckline, at a dance or a party? These were the questions to which Allen found himself giving the wrong, or non-Inish, answers, attempting to lift the veil that had covered Druidism for centuries, so that it is not surprising that I began to believe less and less in his business expertise búsquelas en nuestras tiendas and equally little in his reminiscences of Pilkington Mrs. D., neither an affirmation nor a denial, and pay more attention to my good friend Mr. H. Jacet, who was particularly sympathetic regarding my son Deo.

"You should try to get him into a good womb", he advised, flying his buttons across the old stationmaster's old office with an underarm flick of his umbrella: "There are several nicer wombs in this nicer suburb which I am sure would suit you. Would you like me to make some discreet enquiries? I have some particulars here, as a matter of fact"—he opened his copy of tomorrow's *Times*, they call all these local rags the and began to read: "Accommodation comprises: entrance porch and wide hall . . .", but at the time, not being certain of my immediate plans I interrupted him, telling him I had no immediate plans for my son Deo but was just looking round for a likely . . .

"Ah yes, I understand—quite so", he agreed modestly,

as one to whom such things were a matter of breeding. "You will want to know the district a little better. Today we continue our service for new readers, and each tomorrow on this page we publish a list of events which will help you plan yours. We will also suggest tours that can be made by car, bus, on bicycle or on foot".

"It is a pleasant country", I had replied, "I like it—your people are so friendly, your girls, so charming, your paysage, so unspoilt, your . . .".

"Wombs of character in all districts", Mr. Jacet was continuing, "a very considerable sum has been spent on modernising this property without taking away from its old-world charm. Part oil-fired central heating installed. The property has very great charm and character".

But though I had recognised the description of Pilkington, Mrs. D., even Mr. H. Jacet's final attempt at persuasion ("This property must be seen to be appreciated") could not at that time win my attention from the occasional glimpses of Miss Nicer O'Pair Girl, who had taken off most of her and the problem of my son Deo, he of the pure phonemes, he of the unassailable background, he of the written history (Insularity in its Contemporary Manifestations) which was shelved alongside the sardine tin that I had inherited with the old stationmaster's old office.

"Which leaves nobody but yourself".

Z 3 had taken up his old position by the fireplace, his feathers plucked and scattered, his bony index sucked clean of the last traces of sardine oil.

"It's time you were getting the traps together", he was saying, "if I'm to leave you down in time. The lads will be here any minute, and they won't be best pleased if you're still sitting on them trying to get the lids closed.

•

Anyway I suppose you'll want to be slipping out on to the platform for a few minutes just to take a last look round. It's always a hard thing to say goodbye to a place—even if it's a place you hate the sight of. If I were you now I'd be getting those papers tucked in and bedded down— they might easily get forgotten at the last minute".

He was right, as usual. For the past four years next March, next March being a leap year, I had been stalling for time, trying to hand it to myself as casually as possible, and now that it was all over I could hardly bring myself to finish the advertisement and make an end of it. But I had just checked the timetable 8.06 / 8.36 / 9.06 / and it was time, at last time to be going. I wound myself up for the last of the farewell speeches we'd been making to one another, but he was draining the sardine tin now, and I suddenly noticed the deepening lines on his cheeks and the black-pepper pattern of stubble, things you're always supposed to be noticing if you're observant or a woman but that I never register in the ordinary way of things. "Well, it's been good, Ecks", he led off, or some simple banality like that, as I picked up my traps and began to move out the door towards the gangway. The canvas sides were flapping horribly, and the officers mounting guard were holding their hats on in the wind as if frozen into an everlasting forelock-touching posture. I had forgotten how foul the weather had been when I disembarked four years ago next March being and I had forgotten how many arracks we had drunk, myself and Ecks and Mr. H. Jacet and Allen and Señorita Hermosilla Jacet (whom I might say I do not see coming down the gangplank with seven and a half inches and) and Pilkington Mrs. D. so that now the mixture of cold-air-condi-

tioning and hot railway wind hit me in the stomach like a
blow from the handle of a push-and-pull lawnmower when
it jams on one of the dog's bones, as the domesticated Mr.
H. Jacet more than once had occasion to remark, and I
fought back, won by a hairsbreadth from the prickly bile
taste that washed my back teeth and I was just about to
go out through the door of the old stationmaster's old office, putting my hand in my raincoat, touching the reassuring bulk of tomorrow's local when Z 3 called to me
from his position by the fire, in which the old timetables—
or was it Sir John Daniel?—were still smouldering.

"All persons not travelling please board the tender by
the Entrance on Platform One", he called, and I stopped.
Of course, I was going the wrong way. And then, just as I
turned to go back into the old stationmaster's old office,
hoping to close my eyes, to try for an easy take-off into
suspended animation, hands on pullover inside raincoat
through double pockets, ankles crossed as if chained, the
lads arrived to help with the traps. I noticed with some
surprise how powerful their arms looked.

Bernard Share is a distinguished critic, writer, and teacher. He is a former editor of *Cara*, the Aer Lingus in-flight magazine, and the author of many books, including the bestselling *The Emergency*, a popular account of Irish life during World War II, and the novel *Transit*. Share has been a lecturer in modern literature both in Ireland and Australia.

The John F. Byrne Irish Literature Series is made possible through a generous contribution by an anonymous individual. This contribution will allow Dalkey Archive Press to publish one book per year in this series.

Born and raised in Chicago, John F. Byrne was an educator and critic who helped to found the *Review of Contemporary Fiction* and was also an editor for Dalkey Archive Press. Although his primary interest was Victorian literature, he spent much of his career teaching modern literature, especially such Irish writers as James Joyce, Samuel Beckett, and Flann O'Brien. He died in 1998, but his influence on both the *Review* and Dalkey Archive Press will be lasting.

SELECTED DALKEY ARCHIVE PAPERBACKS

FOR A FULL LIST OF PUBLICATIONS, VISIT:
www.dalkeyarchive.com

SELECTED DALKEY ARCHIVE PAPERBACKS

HARRY MATHEWS,
The Case of the Persevering Maltese: Collected Essays.
Cigarettes.
The Conversions.
The Human Country: New and Collected Stories.
The Journalist.
My Life in CIA.
Singular Pleasures.
The Sinking of the Odradek Stadium.
Tlooth.
20 Lines a Day.
ROBERT L. MCLAUGHLIN, ED.,
Innovations: An Anthology of Modern &
Contemporary Fiction.
HERMAN MELVILLE, *The Confidence-Man.*
AMANDA MICHALOPOULOU, *I'd Like.*
STEVEN MILLHAUSER, *The Barnum Museum.*
In the Penny Arcade.
RALPH J. MILLS, JR., *Essays on Poetry.*
OLIVE MOORE, *Spleen.*
NICHOLAS MOSLEY, *Accident.*
Assassins.
Catastrophe Practice.
Children of Darkness and Light.
Experience and Religion.
God's Hazard.
The Hesperides Tree.
Hopeful Monsters.
Imago Bird.
Impossible Object.
Inventing God.
Judith.
Look at the Dark.
Natalie Natalia.
Paradoxes of Peace.
Serpent.
Time at War.
The Uses of Slime Mould: Essays of Four Decades.
WARREN MOTTE,
Fables of the Novel: French Fiction since 1990.
Fiction Now: The French Novel in the 21st Century.
Oulipo: A Primer of Potential Literature.
YVES NAVARRE, *Our Share of Time.*
Sweet Tooth.
DOROTHY NELSON, *In Night's City.*
Tar and Feathers.
WILFRIDO D. NOLLEDO, *But for the Lovers.*
FLANN O'BRIEN, *At Swim-Two-Birds.*
At War.
The Best of Myles.
The Dalkey Archive.
Further Cuttings.
The Hard Life.
The Poor Mouth.
The Third Policeman.
CLAUDE OLLIER, *The Mise-en-Scène.*
PATRIK OUŘEDNÍK, *Europeana.*
FERNANDO DEL PASO, *News from the Empire.*
Palinuro of Mexico.
ROBERT PINGET, *The Inquisitory.*
Mahu or The Material.
Trio.
MANUEL PUIG, *Betrayed by Rita Hayworth.*
RAYMOND QUENEAU, *The Last Days.*
Odile.
Pierrot Mon Ami.
Saint Glinglin.
ANN QUIN, *Berg.*
Passages.
Three.
Tripticks.
ISHMAEL REED, *The Free-Lance Pallbearers.*
The Last Days of Louisiana Red.
Reckless Eyeballing.
The Terrible Threes.
The Terrible Twos.
Yellow Back Radio Broke-Down.
JEAN RICARDOU, *Place Names.*
RAINER MARIA RILKE,
The Notebooks of Malte Laurids Brigge.
JULIÁN RÍOS, *Larva: A Midsummer Night's Babel.*
Poundemonium.
AUGUSTO ROA BASTOS, *I the Supreme.*
OLIVIER ROLIN, *Hotel Crystal.*
JACQUES ROUBAUD, *The Form of a City Changes Faster,*
Alas, Than the Human Heart.
The Great Fire of London.
Hortense in Exile.
Hortense Is Abducted.
The Loop.
The Plurality of Worlds of Lewis.
The Princess Hoppy.
Some Thing Black.
LEON S. ROUDIEZ, *French Fiction Revisited.*

VEDRANA RUDAN, *Night.*
LYDIE SALVAYRE, *The Company of Ghosts.*
Everyday Life.
The Lecture.
The Power of Flies.
LUIS RAFAEL SÁNCHEZ, *Macho Camacho's Beat.*
SEVERO SARDUY, *Cobra & Maitreya.*
NATHALIE SARRAUTE, *Do You Hear Them?*
Martereau.
The Planetarium.
ARNO SCHMIDT, *Collected Stories.*
Nobodaddy's Children.
CHRISTINE SCHUTT, *Nightwork.*
GAIL SCOTT, *My Paris.*
DAMION SEARLS, *What We Were Doing and Where We*
Were Going.
JUNE AKERS SEESE,
Is This What Other Women Feel Too?
What Waiting Really Means.
BERNARD SHARE, *Inish.*
Transit.
AURELIE SHEEHAN, *Jack Kerouac Is Pregnant.*
VIKTOR SHKLOVSKY, *Knight's Move.*
A Sentimental Journey: Memoirs 1917–1922.
Energy of Delusion: A Book on Plot.
Literature and Cinematography.
Theory of Prose.
Third Factory.
Zoo, or Letters Not about Love.
JOSEF ŠKVORECKÝ,
The Engineer of Human Souls.
CLAUDE SIMON, *The Invitation.*
GILBERT SORRENTINO, *Aberration of Starlight.*
Blue Pastoral.
Crystal Vision.
Imaginative Qualities of Actual Things.
Mulligan Stew.
Pack of Lies.
Red the Fiend.
The Sky Changes.
Something Said.
Splendide-Hôtel.
Steelwork.
Under the Shadow.
W. M. SPACKMAN, *The Complete Fiction.*
GERTRUDE STEIN, *Lucy Church Amiably.*
The Making of Americans.
A Novel of Thank You.
PIOTR SZEWC, *Annihilation.*
STEFAN THEMERSON, *Hobson's Island.*
The Mystery of the Sardine.
Tom Harris.
JEAN-PHILIPPE TOUSSAINT, *The Bathroom.*
Camera.
Monsieur.
Television.
DUMITRU TSEPENEAG, *Pigeon Post.*
The Necessary Marriage.
Vain Art of the Fugue.
ESTHER TUSQUETS, *Stranded.*
DUBRAVKA UGRESIC, *Lend Me Your Character.*
Thank You for Not Reading.
MATI UNT, *Brecht at Night*
Diary of a Blood Donor.
Things in the Night.
ÁLVARO URIBE AND OLIVIA SEARS, EDS.,
The Best of Contemporary Mexican Fiction.
ELOY URROZ, *The Obstacles.*
LUISA VALENZUELA, *He Who Searches.*
PAUL VERHAEGHEN, *Omega Minor.*
MARJA-LIISA VARTIO, *The Parson's Widow.*
BORIS VIAN, *Heartsnatcher.*
AUSTRYN WAINHOUSE, *Hedyphagetica.*
PAUL WEST, *Words for a Deaf Daughter & Gala.*
CURTIS WHITE, *America's Magic Mountain.*
The Idea of Home.
Memories of My Father Watching TV.
Monstrous Possibility: An Invitation to
Literary Politics.
Requiem.
DIANE WILLIAMS, *Excitability: Selected Stories.*
Romancer Erector.
DOUGLAS WOOLF, *Wall to Wall.*
Ya! & John-Juan.
JAY WRIGHT, *Polynomials and Pollen.*
The Presentable Art of Reading Absence.
PHILIP WYLIE, *Generation of Vipers.*
MARGUERITE YOUNG, *Angel in the Forest.*
Miss MacIntosh, My Darling.
REYOUNG, *Unbabbling.*
ZORAN ŽIVKOVIĆ, *Hidden Camera.*
LOUIS ZUKOFSKY, *Collected Fiction.*
SCOTT ZWIREN, *God Head.*

FOR A FULL LIST OF PUBLICATIONS, VISIT:
www.dalkeyarchive.com